THE SEASON FOR KISSING

"Where are your gloves?" he asked. "You—"

"A serious man," Olivia interrupted, "would not over-set his aunt by unexpectedly inviting hordes of children to her party." She gave him a severe look. "A serious man would not let Susanna run amok with a kissing bough."

"I'm afraid I have no control over—"

She tilted her chin down; her bright eyes steady on his own. Her free hand came up to prod at cravat again, so he captured that one, too. Her brows came together, but her eyes remained locked with his. "A serious man would not let his lady guests kiss him."

He jerked back, wounded. "I protest. Miss Faraday, I have not—"

Her pretty lips curved into an utterly innocent, utterly captivating smile. "But you are not serious," she whispered.

And then she rose quickly on her toes and pressed her mouth briefly to his. . . .

Books by Catherine Blair

THE SCANDALOUS MISS DELANEY

THE HERO RETURNS

ATHENA'S CONQUEST

A FAMILY FOR GILLIAN

A PERFECT MISMATCH

A SCHOLARLY GENTLEMAN

A VISCOUNT FOR CHRISTMAS

Published by Zebra Books

A VISCOUNT FOR CHRISTMAS

Catherine Blair

ZEBRA BOOKS
Kensington Publishing Corp.
http://www.kensingtonbooks.com

One

Frederica stood at the top of the stairs and spread her arms wide. "I," she announced with all the hauteur a thirteen-year-old could muster, "am going to be married."

Olivia braced the breakfast tray against her hip and looked up at her sister. "Excellent," she said. "I'm delighted to hear it. I hope he will be very rich and *very* indulgent. We shan't have any meat for Sunday dinner if we don't find a way to pay the butcher's bill."

She looked down at the tray she held and grimaced. Perhaps Papa would be eating better if he had more appealing food. He'd hardly touched the porridge and currant buns she'd prepared for him. And didn't he know how dear currants were this time of year? Perhaps luncheon would be better received.

Frederica descended the stairs, posed like the regal women depicted in the batch of last year's fashion plates the dowager Lady Harrow had condescended to give them. "My husband will be very rich indeed. We shall have meat every day. And not just chicken, either." She rolled her eyes in anticipation. "We shall have a Christmas pudding and gingerbread and chocolate and sugarplums and all the spiced punch we can drink."

Olivia refrained from reminding her sister not to walk

down the middle of the stair runner to save the carpet. Instead she offered Freddie Papa's spurned currant bun. "I daresay we shall all have stomachaches," she said dryly.

She carried Papa's tray into the kitchen and set about tidying up. Frederica followed her and reluctantly began to help.

Olivia watched her sister's rough hands competently scrape Papa's leavings onto the plate to be given to Trueheart, the last of the hunting dogs left in the empty stable. She felt the familiar raw burn of irritation. Frederica should be practicing the harp, learning impractical foreign languages, painting pastoral Christmas scenes in watercolor. She should be learning the skills that would ensure that her mock announcement of a brilliant match could someday become something like reality.

"I *am* going to marry someone rich, you know," her sister said, as though she could read Olivia's thoughts. "And he'll make sure that Papa is seen by the very best doctors, and he'll buy us all the clothes we could ever want. A new gown for every day of the year. And he'll see to Susanna and the boys, and you, too, of course."

"Generous man," Olivia muttered.

Molly, their maid of all work, bustled in with a bucket of water from the pump. It was already fringed with ice around the edges.

"I'm sorry, miss. I didn't realize you were finished. Do you need help with Mr. Faraday?" She strained to lift the water and pour it into the big kettle on the hob. Olivia went to help her.

"No, thank you, Molly. I'll just push his chair into the study. You know he's waiting for my sister's arrival. He can watch for her from there."

Perhaps things would be easier once Susanna arrived

home with her two young sons. It would mean more mouths, but more hands as well. She found herself totting up the bills, the savings, the lessening trickle of income. The numbers clicked and rattled in her head like worry beads.

She felt her heart beginning to pound harder in panic and forced herself to turn around and focus on the leftover food that must be made up again for luncheon, the wood she must ask Willard to cut, the dunning letters that must be written for the few last outstanding agricultural projects her father had completed. The list was so long.

The maid nodded. "I'm sorry about Miss Susanna's husband passing on so sudden-like, but I'm glad she's coming home with the children. Poor lambs need to be with family. And it will be good for you to have some help in taking care of Mr. Faraday. If you don't mind me saying so, you're looking peaky these days. It's too much for one person. When I think of how things used to be when young Mr. Christopher was alive, and how you girls—"

"I know, I know," Olivia snapped. She smoothed her hair more securely into its tight chignon and stood up straighter. "However, things are the way they are. Anyway, Frederica is a great help, and Susanna will be able to lend a hand, as you say."

She gave the girl a brisk smile, but she saw the maid's look of pity before she turned away. Molly was good to stay with them. But the idea that she did it because she felt sorry for the Faraday family was lowering.

Olivia knew she couldn't dwell on matters of family pride. Heavens, they couldn't even afford that. Ever since they'd had news of her brother Christopher's death in Spain last year, her father's health had declined. He was frail now, and absentminded. But perhaps things would be better now that Susanna was coming home.

"There's Christmas just around the corner," Molly continued, undaunted. "That should cheer everyone up."

Olivia resisted the urge to throw up her hands in despair. Christmas! She didn't have time for Christmas. Since her father had been too ill to work, they had had to live off the small income from his investments. She didn't have the time, money, or heart to think about fripperies like holly and ivy.

Frederica danced along behind her toward the drawing room, where Papa had spent the morning enjoying the winter sunlight. "Do you know who I'm going to marry, Olivia?" she asked, obviously enjoying spinning out the suspense.

"No." She was about to state sharply that she had more important things to attend to than fantasy weddings, but a look at her sister's innocent, hopeful face and she bit back her response. "Who? Who would you like to marry?"

Her sister slipped in front of her and blocked the doorway to the drawing room with a dramatic pose. "Lord Harrow."

Olivia made a face and rolled her eyes. "Harrow? You mean the old viscount's heir? Oh really, Freddie, that's ridiculous."

Lord Harrow indeed. The whole world knew he was the most irresponsible, pleasure-mad, sponging housebent, ineligible bachelor London had to offer. Their only consolation in inheriting the dilettante as landlord and employer last year was that the modest little hamlet of Littleton had hardly been exciting enough to entice him to visit.

"Olivia!" her father's voice came from somewhere

behind Frederica. "Where are you, girl? It's too cold in here. Why don't you have a proper fire built up?"

Olivia went to him, making soothing assurances. Despite the wheeled chair, Papa was still an imposing figure—tall and straight, topped with a colossus of a nose that would make Wellington whimper. But in the last year he had been whittled down to a twig. Oh, if only he'd eat more.

Her father brushed away her words. "Take me to the study. You should be practicing the . . ." he groped for the word, impatiently waving his hand toward the pianoforte in the corner. "The instrument. I don't pay good money for lessons if you don't practice. Monsignor Villafana comes today, you know. No point in having a Frenchman in the house if he ain't a cook or a music teacher. Or perhaps a dancing master. Though we might be able to find you an Italian for that."

Olivia shot her sister a look of warning and went to position herself behind the wheeled chair. She pushed him down the dim hallway, still elegant with drawings and paintings of the great estates he had landscaped and improved. She ticked them off like a roster of the most important personages in the country: the Staffords, the Derbys, the Cavandishes, the Granvilles. They had all vied for her father's services in his day.

He'd been celebrated by the most noble families of England. Their patronage had bought the Faradays their fine paintings, elegant furniture, impressive stables, and genteel educations. It had given them all the trappings of the landed gentry. And Papa had spent beyond his means to ensure they had those trappings.

Their mounting debts hadn't mattered until Christopher died on the battlefield. Then things had changed. There was no one to carry on with Papa's work, no heir to the entailed estates from their uncle Faraday. And her father himself seemed to have changed. Perhaps it wouldn't have been right for him to take on new projects while he was in mourning. But it wasn't that. The man had somehow lost his focus.

Even those projects that had formerly interested him no longer seemed to flourish under his hands. These days Papa was forever mislaying plans, losing blueprints, forgetting which of his patrons had requested what. The honorable Miss Hortense Merrywell had sent back his plans for her new summerhouse with a terse letter saying that she'd explicitly stated earlier that she didn't want pediments.

"Monsignor Villafona stopped coming to the house a year ago," she reminded him gently.

"A year?" her father looked insulted. "Damned Frenchmen are always late."

Perhaps things would improve. After all, they'd lain off blacks months ago. It was time to put Christopher's death aside and move on.

"Why shouldn't I marry Lord Harrow?" Frederica demanded, her pretty, round face puckered into a pout. "He's rich, and handsome, and he's not so terribly old."

The heir was likely a good ten years older than Frederica, perhaps a year or two older than Olivia's twenty years. But if the stories were true, he acted like a boy still green from the university.

"Yes," Olivia said caustically, "and doubtless he's just itching to find an opportunity to marry the impoverished daughter of his uncle's estate manager." She navigated the unwieldy bath chair around the spindly gilt chairs and inlaid tables of the study and stopped near the window. "I'll start planning the wedding breakfast immediately. I do hope the guests won't expect currant buns."

Frederica looked up at her, tears immediately springing to her eyes. "I don't understand how you can be so horrid, Olivia. You didn't used to be so awful. Nowadays you can't say a single kind thing to anyone." She drew herself up and squared her thin shoulders. "We're a respectable family. Papa is an agricultural consultant, not an estate manager. You always used to say there was a world of difference. And you and Susanna had proper Seasons in London. And Susanna married a captain. There's nothing wrong with us. It's simply not fair that we should become poor before I should get a chance to make a brilliant match."

Olivia sighed, instantly ashamed. "I'm sorry, Freddie. I shouldn't have said what I did." It *wasn't* fair. Things had been very different when she and Susanna were her age.

"And besides," Frederica went on doggedly, "if Lord Harrow did happen to want to marry me, it would solve everything."

"Monsignor Villafona," her father mused. "Yes. Never liked the man much. But he is a great musician. Taught all four of you. Of course, Christopher was too impatient, and Susanna too silly. Olivia, you are the only one who shows any promise. Which is a good thing, girl. You haven't the looks to make a match if you don't play pianoforte. You likely should take up the harp as well."

Olivia glanced at her reflection in the mirror over the hearth. Her father was right, of course. She was no beauty. Unlike the slender, fair Susanna, she was too skinny and too pale. Her hair, while abundant, was wildly ordinary in color, and her eyes were too light a blue to be considered pretty. She was nothing offensive, but certainly didn't have looks enough to overcome her obvious shortfalls in breeding and wealth.

She turned back to her father, slightly relieved that he was talking sensibly at last. He didn't always these days. "Susanna and the children won't be arriving for hours, Papa. Are you certain you wish to sit here and look out for them?"

"Of course," he snapped. "Want to keep an eye on the weather. It looks like it might snow. First snow of the year. It would be just like Susanna to start out in a snow-storm." He rocked the chair closer to the window and squinted up at the sky, his eyes a startling blue in the morning light. "Though I do think it will hold off until tomorrow." He settled back into the chair and smiled. "Now, you run along and amuse yourself, Olivia."

She dropped a kiss on his cheek and smiled. There were the menus to be done and the guest rooms to be aired out in preparation for her sister and the boys. Molly would need help with luncheon, and someone had to go to the market for tomorrow's dinner. She couldn't remember the last time she had amused herself.

Frederica helped her tuck a blanket around Papa's thin knees. Her sister wore a wounded expression, her eyes carefully averted.

Olivia regretted speaking so sharply to her. After all, a girl was allowed to dream. It had been unkind of her to dismiss her sister's childish plans to save them all by marrying the lord of the grand estate.

"There is no need for you to sacrifice yourself to someone so unworthy as Lord Harrow," she said, taking her sister's arm and settling the old lace fichu the girl had inexpertly pinned around her neckline. "We shall get along tolerably well, and when the time comes, you will make a very fine love match with someone who is worthy of the daughter of the famous Mr. Faraday."

She smoothed her sister's plaits. "Now, come to the

butcher's shop with me. Molly will make certain Papa has everything he needs. It will do you good to get some air. And you can gather some greenery on the way back to make the Christmas garlands you were talking about."

"I hear he's very handsome," Frederica said, twitching out from under her sister's ministrations. "I don't think I would mind marrying him at all. And I would be very rich."

"I doubt it," Olivia said, then, hearing the bitterness in her voice, she forced a laugh. "Harrow will have wasted the whole of his fortune before he's thirty. You wouldn't want to be saddled with that, now would you?"

Frederica did not look dissuaded. In fact, her chin was taking on a decidedly stubborn look. "I *do* want to marry him," she said. "It's my Christmas wish. You've always said that everyone deserves one special Christmas wish. And mine always come true. Remember last year I wished that Trueheart would have puppies? And the year before when I wished that I would draw queen on Twelfth Night? They always come true. And I've decided I want to marry Lord Harrow."

A Christmas wish. Had she ever been so idealistic?

"Come on, Freddie," Olivia said with a sigh. "Let's go to the shops."

"Yes, yes," said her father, unexpectedly drawing his eyes away from the window. "You girls need some air. Take Willard and go for a drive in Littleton Park. Harrow likes to see you girls use it, you know."

Olivia smiled and pretended she hadn't heard correctly. Beauford Harrow, her father's old crony, had been dead more than a year. The loss of his patronage, coupled with Christopher's death on the continent, had been the beginning of their troubles.

She pulled Frederica toward the kitchen. It wasn't fair

to let her younger sister see her worries. And Freddie was right. She'd been out of sorts of late.

But perhaps Papa would be better soon, and then perhaps things would go back to how they had been. If she herself had any Christmas wish, it was that.

"Molly, could you please make certain Papa is looked after?" she asked, taking her cloak and bonnet from the peg in the kitchen. "Frederica and I must go to the butcher's shop now, if we wish to be back before Susanna arrives. Though Lord knows she'll likely be late."

It would be good to see Susanna again. And the twins—heavens, they must be all of five or six by now. Poor Susanna, to lose her brother and then her husband all in a twelvemonth. Indeed, the Faraday family had had a difficult year. It would be comforting to be together for Christmas, even though the circumstances weren't the happiest.

"It will be lovely to have a handsome viscount for a husband," Frederica mused. "I don't care if he is prostilgate."

"Profligate," Olivia corrected dryly. "Very well, Freddie, we'll consider it a Christmas wish." She stepped out the door and drew in a breath of cold air. "Now. Tell me how it is that you intend to woo our father's new employer, that paragon, Lord Harrow."

Two

Olivia and Frederica strode across the lawn and crossed the road to cut through Reverend Eggart's field. Better to muddy their boots and the hems of their skirts than to take too long about the errands. Papa got cross when they were gone and often didn't recall that there was no one else but Molly to help with the running of the house.

Besides, the quick trot helped ward off the chill. Olivia watched her breath condense in a thick plume and mentally calculated how much coal they'd need to keep Papa warm if the winter turned out unusually long and cold.

Frederica was still going on about her ridiculous viscount.

"Do you think I can have a new gown made up for the Harrows' Christmas ball? There's bound to be one, don't you think? It would be such a shame if they didn't have one. Though perhaps they won't, since the dowager is only just out of mourning. The new viscount will come for Christmas, don't you think? I mean, he must come at some point."

"He hasn't yet," Olivia reminded her. "Papa has completed improvements for people who never even saw them. And after all, the estate brings Harrow money, which he can more conveniently waste in London. Why

would he wish to inspect his goose as long as it contin-
ues to lay golden eggs?" She hitched the basket more
securely on her arm and wrapped her cloak tighter
around her. She didn't remember a December so cold.
Oh, how would they ever pay for coal until spring?

"You're so cyndrical."

"Cynical," she corrected. Had she always been cynical? She couldn't recall. Gracious, she was getting as
bad as Papa.

Their boots crunched across the frozen grass in silence
for a moment. "I met Harrow once, you know," she said.
It was silly. Silly that she'd even remember it.

Frederica looked at her as though she'd announced
she'd flown to the moon once. "And was he handsome?"

"Yes." She gave a rueful shrug, wishing it weren't
true. But he had been. Noticeably so. Or at least she had
thought so at the time. It had been a good two years
since that one London Season. That one excruciating,
painful humiliation of a Season. After all, the daughter
of an agricultural consultant was hardly likely to receive
the best invitations. And even at those fetes she did attend, she couldn't really be expected to be noticed.
Certainly not by a man as handsome as Jack Harrow.

"Was he charming? Did he speak with you?"

"No," she said definitively. "He was introduced to me
once, and he shook my hand while looking around the
room for someone more interesting to talk to. Aunt
Sarah hinted that perhaps I would like to dance the next
set, but Harrow merely took himself off to the card
room. He was not, by any stretch of the imagination,
what one might call charming."

"But he *is* handsome," Frederica insisted, obviously
unwilling to abandon her plan entirely. "And rich. Particularly now."

Olivia picked her way across the muddy patch in front of the stile. "I suppose," she granted, climbing over it, "though I suspect like many men, he's been living beyond his means for years. I expect he'll squeeze what he can out of the estate, then let it go to ruin. He's your typical town buck. Mad for sporting, gambling, fine clothes, and any amusement. He hasn't likely got a single original thought in his head."

"But he *is* handsome," Frederica said again, clambering over the stile behind her.

Olivia hoped that Susanna's boys were not big eaters. There was no way they could reasonably afford to feed three more people.

Perhaps though, Susanna would be their salvation. Olivia had written her sister a carefully worded letter in an attempt to find out if Captain Clarke had left anything to his young widow, but Susanna hadn't answered. Frankly, Olivia hadn't much hope regarding the situation of a half-pay officer who'd had the misfortune to die of a liver complaint instead of the battlefield.

She shrugged. "Dress any man in a fine suit of clothes and he is handsome. No, Frederica, I'm afraid you would find Harrow a great disappointment."

Her spirit not the least bit dampened, Frederica followed her down the lane. "Molly said that the groom at the Blue Hen said that he drives a four-in-hand."

"Likely so."

They entered the butcher's shop. The aroma of ham baking in the back room hit Olivia in a warm, fragrant cloud. Her stomach rumbled.

Mr. Yarborough came out from the back, wiping his hands on his apron. She tried not to consider what the various stains on it might be.

"I've decorated the shop for Christmas," he announced,

his ruddy face shiny from the heat of the roasting ovens. "There's some folk who don't like to see bits of holly stuck in their chops, but I can't see the harm."

"No, indeed," Olivia agreed. She wondered how she might hint that his baked hams might need an unbiased bystander to taste their progress.

"And," Frederica went on, gesturing broadly to indicate that her comments were far more important than wistfully eyeing the flock of plump and naked geese lined up on the sideboard, "Molly said that the groom said that Harrow might come to Littleton Park for Christmas. Despite what you think. She said his aunt wrote him and invited him to spend the whole of the holidays here."

"Likely because he's being dunned in town." Olivia tried to think back to the man she had met so briefly in the long-ago days when she made her bow. He'd been like so many other men: handsome, privileged—their polite veneer barely masking their scorn at being introduced to the daughter of an agriculturalist. A memory snagged in her mind. "When I met him I believe he was engaged."

"No," Frederica said in a tone of great authority. "He was engaged to Miss Ophelia D'Ore. But she cried off. That was ages ago. Now Lord Harrow is entirely unattached."

Olivia took the joint of meat she'd ordered yesterday, signed the alarmingly long list of items to be billed, and then settled her treasure in her basket. She tried to recall the last time they'd had more than slivers of mutton or stringy chicken for their dinner. Lord Harrow and his ilk might turn up their noses at this modest cut of beef, but she was looking forward to the feast with relish.

"Are you talking about the new viscount?" Mr.

Yarborough asked. "I hear he's accepted his aunt's command to come to see her over Christmas."

Frederica gave a piercing shriek. "See?" she squealed triumphantly. "My Christmas wish is coming true. He is coming for Christmas, and I will get to meet him."

Olivia exchanged an indulgent smile with Mr. Yarborough. A little fantasy would do her sister no harm. There was little likelihood of the viscount developing designs on a country girl not yet out of the schoolroom. Perhaps it was wrong of her to have been so repressive about Harrow. After all, wasn't it every girl's right to dream of a prince who would win her heart and solve all her problems?

Mr. Yarborough grinned and slyly added a length of sausage to the basket on the counter. "I daresay he'll want to have a grand Christmas ball. The gentry in London always have something fancy-like."

The butcher chuckled at Frederica's delighted exclamation. "Now don't get too excited about it, Miss Frederica," he protested. "The dowager isn't likely to approve. She isn't the sort to host any big kickup in the first place, and certainly not when she's just out of mourning. She'll make sure nothing comes of it. Any Christmas festivities here will be nothing like what he's used to in London, leastways." He patted the row of geese with great affection. "I hear there, Lord Harrow once won a bet that he could drink more glasses of champagne than his age."

Olivia sniffed. She had more important things on her mind than the drinking, gambling, and carousing habits of London dandies.

The butcher made an elaborate show of drawing out his watch from behind his apron. "My brother works as an underbutler at Littleton Park, and he said Lord Harrow is expected there today." He gave a roar of laughter at Freddie's shrill scream. "I hear the viscount drives a phaeton with a perch six feet high. Can you imagine that coming through the street? Though he'd likely be frozen to a solid block of ice on a day like today."

Frederica ran to the window as though she expected to see the carriage that very moment. "Olivia, I'm not stirring from this spot until I see him," she announced. "They'll have to have a ball, wouldn't you think? And if they do, they'll have to invite us. Papa would let me go, wouldn't he? Or perhaps I could ride out and contrive to have a fall just when he is out riding and Harrow could rescue me. That would work out very well, wouldn't you think?"

Olivia smiled. After all, Christmas wishes were Christmas wishes.

"Did those Faradays pay their bill from last month?" Mrs. Yarborough shouted from the back.

Mr. Yarborough shot Olivia a look of pity, then pretended to be very absorbed in the contents of the salted beef barrel.

"Next week, Mrs. Yarborough," she called out, her face painfully hot. "My sister is coming from London today."

That implied, perhaps incorrectly, that Susanna would have the funds to pay the bill, but there was a slight chance that it wasn't a falsehood.

Suddenly Frederica gave a wild shriek. "He's coming! I see the carriage!"

"Stop funning, Freddie."

"I'm not! It's really him!" Before Olivia could point out that even if it really was the viscount, racing into the street and gawping like a gutter child was hardly the way to impress him, her sister had grabbed her forcibly by the elbow and dragged her out of the shop. The icy wind hit them with eye-watering force, and they had a fleeting glimpse of a bottle-blue curricle pulled by a matched white team.

Frederica barely had time to release an exuberant sigh of love before they were splattered liberally with a cold dash of muddy water.

Olivia looked down at her damaged cloak. A deep blue edged in black fur, it had been fashionable in its day. Well, it had seen more than a bit of mud since then. And perhaps this would teach her not to get too attached to the trappings of the past.

She looked up to give the carriage driver a look of disgust and was surprised to see that it had stopped not far up the road. One of the figures in the curricle turned around and gave a squeal.

"Olivia! Freddie! Lud, is that you?"

"Is that Susanna?" Frederica gasped. "With Lord Harrow?"

Olivia walked a few steps toward them, not entirely sure that the fantastically garbed woman waving at her was indeed their sister.

"Olivia! What a laugh that it should be you! I was just saying to Lord Harrow that it would be only perfect if someone I knew should see me arrive home in such style. Am I not quite grand?" She stood up in the seat and gestured to her gown, the carriage, and the man beside her.

Olivia could not help but smile. All were, indeed, quite grand. Susanna, the eldest and always the acknowledged family beauty, was dressed in mourning as appropriate to a widow of only six months. But her gown had obviously been cut by London's most fashionable modiste. The carriage was the first kick of style, and her escort, well, he completed the picture.

The man wore his driving coat with as many capes as possible crammed onto it. His hat was fresh-from-the-box glossy, and the handsome face beneath it just as perfectly sculpted as though it had come to life from a piece of Greek statuary. Her memory of his looks had dulled, evidently. Had he always possessed dark, golden-brown curls that swept across his broad forehead and such a confident, athletic carriage? She branded his open smile slightly vacuous.

Susanna appeared to recall her manners at last. "Lord Harrow, these are my sisters, Miss Olivia Faraday, and Miss Frederica Faraday."

Olivia curtseyed, aware that she'd just further deepened the ring of mud trimming her hem. She really thought she'd forgotten the shame of that London Season. But now the memories of that wretched ordeal hit her with all the force and chill of the north wind. "We met in Town two years ago," she said, with a frosty smile. "Though I don't expect you would recall."

"No," he agreed cheerfully. "I can't recall what I had for breakfast, not to mention something that happened two years ago. However, I'm sure I was shockingly rude to you at the time and rude again now for forgetting it. You must despise me entirely."

Would it be unforgivable to agree? Would the dolt even notice? "Not at all," she said, not even making the effort to smile. Heavens, but she had more important things to think about than pacifying the ego of a pampered town buck. For one thing, she had to get back to Papa.

"Susanna," she said, blurting the first thing her mind could lay hold of, "Papa will be glad to see you. We didn't expect you quite so soon." She realized she was still awkwardly holding her skirts away from her body and dropped the clammy fabric against her legs.

Her sister slanted a glance toward her escort, as though to be certain everyone had admired him appropriately. "Lord Harrow was kind enough to drive me into town. And thank heaven he did. I declare, the mail was positively ghastly. I thought I should die of shame. I don't know what you were thinking, recommending it to me. For all the money I saved, it was crowded, noisy, and positively smelly. Not at all the thing. Were you only teasing me, Olivia? Have I fallen victim to one of your pranks?"

Olivia could not remember if she'd ever played a prank. Particularly when it involved saving a good deal of money.

"Where are your children?" she asked, not a little afraid that her sister had absentmindedly left them behind at the last coaching inn.

Susanna waved a limerick glove in dismissal. "On their way, the little angels. Kitty is coming with them in a hired coach. Really, Olivia, don't look at me that way. I only made it to Hemel Hempstead before I had to hire a carriage. You wouldn't believe the kind of people they allow on the mail. And Lud, it was hung with enough Christmas geese that it looked like Mr. Yarborough's shop on wheels. I thought I should be ill having to look at all those wagging necks outside my window.

"Even once we had hired a carriage, the boys were absolutely incorrigible. I couldn't bear the headache. Anyway, just when I thought I should strangle them like those wretched geese, Lord Harrow came along and rescued me." Her beaming face fell. "Oh, just look at your gown, Olivia! Ruined!"

Olivia forced her own expression to remain neutral. "How kind of Lord Harrow."

She felt Frederica draw a breath beside her and braced herself.

"Welcome to Littleton, my lord. I'm certain you'll enjoy celebrating the holidays with us," her younger sister exclaimed with shrill enthusiasm.

He smiled at them, his handsome face ridiculously convivial. "I—"

"Will you throw a ball?"

Harrow's brows rose slightly. "I hadn't thought about it," he said at last. "I've only just arrived. I don't care for balls overmuch. I'll have to ask my aunt." He gave what might be vulgarly termed a shrug.

The man looked around, assessing with a wrinkled nose the small collection of houses and shops that made up the center of Littleton. "Not much to look at, is it? Can't stand the country, myself. And winter, of course, is the worst. There's not even the redemption of hunting this late in the year."

Susanna laughed as though this were the wittiest thing she'd heard all morning. "Well, la, I'm determined to return home in style. Won't Papa be surprised to see me in this rig-up?" She gave them a cheery wave with her muff. "I'll tell him you're on your way, shall I? Oh, Olivia darling," she called out over her shoulder as the curricle lurched into motion, "could you do me a favor and get me two yards of black grosgrain? I'm simply desperate for it."

Beside her, Olivia heard Frederica give a little sigh. "He's everything elegant, isn't he?" her sister said. "I couldn't think of a single thing to say. And he's far more handsome than I thought, even from what you said. I never saw a man like that in all my life."

Olivia frowned. He hadn't remembered her at all. How silly to have thought he might. She drew herself up and took a firmer grip on the basket containing the precious joint. "I, for one, am unimpressed."

Three

The dowager Lady Harrow put down her teacup and gave another mournful sigh. Jack squinted at the newspaper laid temptingly on the occasional table and wondered if he could possibly read it upside down. His aunt sighed again, this time with violent force, so he was obliged to drag his attention to her. As he had expected, her thin mouth was pulled into a long crescent of displeasure.

"I'm glad you've come, Jack," she said at last.

He forced his own mouth to mobilize into what he hoped was a smile. "Well, er, of course. I wouldn't think of spending Christmas anywhere else."

Except London, or Leicester—where his mother was attending his sister Miriam's second lying-in—or Scotland or China—anywhere would do but here.

He looked around the room, the mirrors still draped with black cloth as though his uncle had given up the ghost moments ago instead of having been in the grave over a year.

Lucky man.

Jack saw that his right foot was tapping a tattoo so impatient that the tassel on his Hessian danced about. He forced himself to still. It wouldn't do to insult Aunt Alva. After all, she was a good sort, and he felt dead guilty about the fact that he'd been the one to inherit instead of Cousin Edward. Though Alva and Beauford had never had children, their nephew Edward had been trained from the cradle for the position as viscount. He'd been everything he should have been: sober, upright, steady, dull. Unfortunately, he'd also been susceptible to inflammation of the lungs.

Poor devil. Though he, too, had escaped Aunt Alva's righteous grasp. Jack wondered briefly if he himself would soon be wishing to stick his spoon in the wall rather than live in this dour place.

His aunt was wearing her pronouncement face, so Jack waited for her to speak. The more momentous the declaration, the longer one had to wait for it. And he had the most disheartening feeling she was not going to announce that she thought it would be great fun if he invited some of his cronies up from town and had a nice, jolly house party with plenty of eating and drinking to relieve the tedium of extensive cardplaying.

Just a wild guess.

He tried to ignore the slow click of the clock, the sound of the fire in the grate and the low murmur of the servants as they cleared up after that painful ordeal that had been dinner. Good Lord, but the country was like a tomb.

"I was considering the matter," Aunt Alva said finally. "And I think it would be best if you started to take some interest in the estate."

He slumped. This was the pronouncement he'd feared.

"Now that Beauford is gone—" She paused to ensure he fully appreciated her loss. "I think it would be best if you moved to Littleton Park and took over your duties as his heir."

Duties. It was really all terribly unfair. Unlike most of his friends who'd have given their eyeteeth for a plumb bit of land, title enough to keep the creditors at bay, and a tidy income, he'd been happy enough as plain Mr. Harrow, care-for-nobody. Now, thanks to the gnarls of the family tree, the fickle hand of fate, and the nasty, putrid fever that took his father, his uncle, and his cousin in the course of one year, he was Viscount Harrow. Possessor of the impressive Littleton Park estate, impressive income, and depressingly impressive duties.

Aunt Alva looked to be as pleased with the situation as himself.

"Duties," he echoed. "Of course." He indulged in the vain hope that Aunt Alva would say that these included the consumption of generous amounts of brandy and the obligation to attend every sporting event mounted. "The estate, you mean?"

"Indeed. The last year has been a shambles. We need an estate manager."

Jack cast about desperately and recalled that his aunt had written something about the existence of an estate manager. "Thought you had one."

She gave a dismissive wave of her thick, beringed hand to indicate that she was about to be modest. "We always had an agricultural consultant, my dear. In recent years, Beauford had Mr. Faraday take care of the estate." She raised her brows in a manner that indicated that he should know the name and be rather impressed.

Faraday. Wasn't the dashing Mrs. Clarke née Faraday? She'd been a laugh. Too flirtatious by half, but good fun anyway. He'd have to be sure she knew he wasn't in the petticoat line. Once she understood he wasn't the marrying kind, she'd train her guns on someone else, and it would all be all right.

Too bad her sisters weren't more like her. One had the face of a child and the other the face of a gorgon.

Oh, she was pretty enough, Miss Faraday, in a common sort of way, but her expression of proud contempt could turn a man to stone. He'd nearly laughed. After all, what did she, with her muddy cloak and her basket of beef, have to be so high-and-mighty about? He'd have been insulted if he hadn't found the whole thing so dashed funny.

"Mr. Faraday is responsible for all the improvements at Lord Derby's Kent estate," his aunt announced, apparently realizing he needed some prompting. "And all the Hertfords' holdings. He's a *gentleman* and Beauford always felt that the estate did very much better under a gentleman agricultural consultant than a mere estate manager. Put Capability Brown in the shade, you know. Far more of an agricultural genius."

She sat back, looking as though she fully expected him to press his hand to his heart and exclaim at her remarkable fortune at securing such a prize. "Unfortunately," she continued when he did not, "Faraday's son died last year, and he was in mourning." She rolled her eyes, marveling at the man's impertinence.

"Ah," he said, attempting to inject his tone with the appropriate amount of knowledge and awe.

The dowager leaned closer, her corsets creaking ominously. "My husband worked very closely with Faraday. He said it was the only way to truly understand the land."

"Ah." Jack closed his eyes and wished himself back to London. He could be there now. Snug in Boodles with the contents of half a bottle warming his stomach and a hunch that the next card would be the one he was waiting for.

"I think it would do you good as well."

"Ah—no!" He drew a sharp breath. "Now, Aunt, you just said the estate affairs are in shambles. You can hardly expect me to pick up the pieces with no one to advise me. Faraday can pick up once he's out of mourning." He stood up and brushed off his trouser legs, hoping this signaled that things were now right and tight, and he was just going to nip off to the billiard room.

Aunt Alva pinned him with a cold stare worthy of the terrifying Miss Faraday herself. He reseated himself immediately. "I was never meant to be landed," he said desperately. "I think it is something I should ease myself into. Safer that way. I should be sure I understand things entirely before I make any decisions. Now then—"

"You'll have to let Faraday go."

He was taken aback for a moment. "I thought you said he was the best."

To his dismay, she put on her tragic expression again and even went so far as to close her eyes for a moment. "Senile," she pronounced dolefully at last. "Beauford ignored it for as long as he could. He was about to dismiss the man when Faraday's only son was killed in Spain. Beauford couldn't bring himself to do it after that. And then, not three weeks later, Beauford himself . . ." She drew a loud breath and held it, apparently to indicate her emotional state.

"I'm sorry, Aunt Alva." It wouldn't be correct to remind his aunt that she had despised her husband while he was among the living. He let the clock click on for a suitable amount of time before he forged on with what must be said. "I think it would be best to hire a new estate manager."

The dowager Lady Harrow expelled her breath in an

explosive huff. "Of course. But it can't be just anyone. Faraday is a genius. You're likely too young to recall it, but he was the most well-known agricultural consultant in his day. He taught Lord Coke all he knew about sheep breeding. He developed his own new strain of swede."

Under the weight of this evidence, Jack managed only a weak smile. "Ah," he said again. Boodles was fading like a pleasant, lost dream.

"The man rents a cottage just down the road. He was a friend to your uncle and knows more about the estate than anyone alive. He—"

"I thought you said he was senile. I thought you said I had to dismiss him."

Aunt Alva skewered him with the Miss Faraday look again. Was there something in the air here that made the women look at him as though he was a three-legged dog with a bad case of mange?

"He has his lucid moments, I believe," she said. "His daughter says he's doing well these days. The creature is in complete denial about his condition. She seems to think he's forgetful merely because of his ill health and because her brother died so tragically. It's nonsense, of course. The man began swearing at Reverend Eggart last week because he thought he was the Prince Regent."

"Faraday thinks he's the Prince Regent?" At least his stay would be interesting.

"No, he thought Reverend Eggart was the Prince Regent," his aunt snapped.

Jack had seen the reverend at his uncle's funeral. Besides corpulence and a penchant for older women, the two did not resemble. "So Faraday's dotty," he confirmed.

His aunt drew herself up to her full height, the black lace on her cap trembling. "Go to him and get all the help from him you can. The man designed the gardens at Darbysham Court; he single-handedly increased wheat production in Sheffield by five percent. Even if half his mind is gone, he can advise a fool like you to run a little place like Littleton Park."

"Well, if that's the case, I don't see why he can't continue to run it," he said with a shrug.

"Impossible. You'll have to get rid of him."

Jack resisted the urge to throw up his hands in defeat. Why couldn't he be like his friends, who were allowed to let their land go to ruin in peace?

"I'll get his advice," he promised. "Perhaps he'll know someone else who can do the job. Or I can go back to London and find someone." Yes, perhaps his brother-in-law Hunter Westhaven knew of someone. Westhaven was a steady sort. He'd sort this out right and tight, and then everything could go on as it had been.

Poor Mr. Faraday. That clever mind sliding away. No wonder his daughter looked so cross. Had the gorgon really met him in London? Surely he would have remembered her. It wasn't every day that one was looked at with such utter loathing. "Did Faraday's daughters have London Seasons?"

At his aunt's expression of surprise, he realized he'd asked the question aloud. He hadn't really meant to. After all, what he really wanted to do was escape to the billiard room, not discuss the roster of young ladies foisted on innocent men every Season.

The lines between his aunt's brows deepened. "I believe they may have. Certainly presumptuous on Faraday's part. He is the best, of course. Though that doesn't entitle him to think his daughters can be encroaching. I do recall, however, that the eldest two daughters had Seasons. Debacles, of course." She gave a satisfied smile for the first time that day. "Why do you ask? Do you know them?"

"No. Well, that is, I believe I may have met Miss Faraday several Seasons ago. Can't imagine where." She didn't look to be the kind of woman who would frequent either society balls or bawdy taverns.

No, Miss Faraday fell into that broad and boring middle ground: genteel, but not a peer; pretty, but not a beauty. The kind of woman who had nothing to recommend herself but a good nature and unblemished reputation had very little to command his attention. And good nature did not appear to be Miss Faraday's strong suit.

"I cannot imagine, either. After all, they were hardly invited anywhere of consequence. The girls had some nobody aunt trotting them out. That was the best they could do." Aunt Alva smoothed the jet fringe on her shawl and looked slightly affronted. "The eldest, who was considered quite a beauty, though I never saw it myself, managed a reasonable match. Quite above her, really. I believe he was in the Tenth Hussars, the Prince's own regiment. A military man, anyway."

"Captain Clarke," he confirmed. "I met Mrs. Clarke on her way home today." No sense telling his aunt he'd been fool enough to offer his carriage to an unchaperoned woman. The dowager might have an apoplectic fit. "Her husband died. Left her with two young sons."

The woman made a noise of vague sympathy, suggesting she'd suspected all along that something like that would occur. "Yes, well, and now she's back at home. And, of course, the other one didn't take at all."

Jack felt a momentary shock of indignation on behalf of Miss Gorgon-Faraday. Then he recalled her look of contempt. "I'm not surprised," he said with an indifferent shrug. "A nobody with more pride than looks or money isn't likely to go far."

His aunt jerked her chin in assent. "I always found her to be unpleasant. Why, even Reverend Eggart said she was a termagant. Though why he was courting her in the first place, I'll never know. Everyone knows he keeps the widow Keller as his mistress. Regardless, the Faraday girl has far too good an opinion of herself if she turned him down. Even if he does drink.

"And—" Aunt Alva drew herself up with another of her dramatic sniffs, "she was positively rude in refusing my invitation that her youngest sister take a position here as a housemaid. After all, I was only trying to help. Lord knows the girl would likely have been a disaster."

Jack resisted the urge to laugh. Poor gorgon. Perhaps she was being punished for her pride. One sister married to a crony of the prince's, the other not good enough to be housemaid. And she in the middle, a nobody. That was rich.

"Beauford always liked her, though," his aunt mused. "I could never fathom why. He said she'd be a beauty. Obviously he was mistaken about that. He said she was too clever to be stuck at home playing nurse to her papa." Perhaps sensing that to admit her husband's lack of judgment was to speak ill of the dead, she stopped herself with a quick sip of tea. "But that's what one must expect, I suppose, when talent raises one's father to his position rather than breeding."

Jack had the rather deflating feeling he didn't want to analyze that sentiment much further. The opposite, after all, had landed him where he was now. Heir to this wretched estate deep in the cold bosom of County Dull.

"Well, they're in a pretty state now," the dowager

said. "Father senile, son dead, and three daughters at home. You'll have to let Faraday go, regardless." She thought for a long moment. "I suppose I'll have to have Cook send them a jelly."

Four

Jack had every intention of explaining politely but firmly to his aunt that if she wanted to rid the estate of old Mr. Faraday, she would have to do it herself. He would trust her to engage a new estate manager whose primary duty would be to leave him alone, and then he would ride back to London with plans never to return. But somehow instead, Jack found himself dismounting in front of the cottage belonging to the Faraday family.

It was a modest house, with noticeably fine gardens. In comparison, the house itself appeared to be in a state of disrepair. It was tidy enough, but could definitely do with a lick of paint and a new roof. Some estate manager, he mused, throwing his reins to the groom, who appeared to be doing double duty as gardener.

Doubtless this would be an unpleasant interview. Breaking bad news to people who didn't deserve it was far outside the realm of his experience. He wished again that he had never inherited the title.

Very well, he would make the visit short. He allowed the rather harassed-looking maid to usher him into a small drawing room and pretended not to notice that she was forced to hastily build a fire in the grate. It was a fine room, rather grand, even. But obviously it had seen better days. The pianoforte had nicked legs and the green brocade silk upholstered chairs had shiny patches of wear on each seat.

Were the Faradays really so badly off then? The pension he'd planned to offer now looked a bit shabby. Perhaps he'd assess just how old and dotty this Mr. Faraday was and either top the pension off a bit or, even better, find that he wasn't half cracked after all and keep him on to manage the estate.

To his surprise it wasn't Faraday who entered the room, but the redoubtable Miss Gorgon. He stifled the urge to laugh. The woman, buttoned up to the chin in a cast-iron bombazine gown, looked him over with a delightfully suspicious eye. "You," she said, in a voice one might use in discovering one's best friend bedding one's expensive new mistress.

"Miss Faraday." He bowed elaborately over her hand. "How pleasant to see you again."

Not that the gorgon maiden was likely to know anything about bedding. Good Lord, under that gown she was probably made of nettles and thorns. Not that the bits and pieces didn't appear to be in all the right places, he noted.

She was pretty enough, but not the kind of voluptuous beauty who might pique his own interest. She was all sharp features, elbows and edges. Striking but severe. He preferred his women more of a round armful. An armful of Miss Faraday would likely leave one with more cuts and bruises than a session at Jackson's boxing salon.

"I'm sorry we're not able to receive you better," she said, a faint blush rising up her cheekbones. "We were not expecting visitors and rarely use this room otherwise. We've been in mourning until recently."

He cast an eye up and down her severe black gown. What she was wearing wasn't mourning? He reminded himself that one didn't ogle ladies. Or even half ladies. Or whatever it was that Miss Faraday was. Besides, perhaps the woman couldn't afford to have new clothes made up.

He shrugged off her apology with a laugh and was rather embarrassed to see a plume of white vapor in the cold air. In the drawing room, for God's sake!

"I should not have descended upon you unexpectedly." Or at least not relinquished his greatcoat when he did so. Surely even Miss Faraday was chilled through her black armor. "But I thought as we're neighbors . . ." He trailed off, feeling like an idiot.

She was more likely to chase neighbors off with a stick than encourage them to drop by. "I do not want to stand on ceremony." He gave her an encouraging smile. "And I brought you a jelly." He offered it out in both hands like a sporting trophy.

He thought for a moment that she was offended. He was struck with the sudden vague recollection that a jelly was the sort of thing one gave to poor people when one was being particularly kind. The fleeting look of hurt that crossed her face cracked her stone-faced hauteur. After a moment, Miss Faraday took the jelly.

"Thank you," she said with dignity.

"And to enquire after your father's health," he added, suddenly nervously jovial. What did he think he was doing here? He wasn't cut out for dispensing largess. Or for putting doddery old estate managers out to pasture.

Not to put too fine a point on it, but he wasn't much cut out for anything. The prickly Miss Faraday, however, didn't look as though she would take this as an excuse.

She drew herself up, her pale blue eyes expressionless. "He's very well, thank you."

Dash it all, but he was a fish out of water. The intrigues of court and the machinations of political parties could be nothing compared to the labyrinthine rules of country gentry. "Excellent, excellent." He heard his voice too loud and too bluff. "It's only that I heard he was ill recently."

Her lips tightened. "Yes, I'm afraid his health has suffered since my brother died."

"I'm very sorry for that." She had a rather nice mouth, but it didn't look appealing, all primed up like that. He cast about in his mind for another topic. "Your sister. How is she?"

He was relieved when she smiled. "Susanna? She does very well. She's turned the house upon its head, of course. And her two sons are clever as monkeys and twice as much trouble. Just this morning, I caught them eating the whole of a pudding Molly had made. They're sick as sailors now, poor things." She laughed, her narrow face suddenly transformed into something a great deal prettier. "I wish I could say they learned a lesson, but of course they have not." She made a comical face. "And Papa is so very keen on plum pudding."

Jack could not help but laugh with her. The woman had a rather dreadful life, by the sound of it, but in a way he envied how she managed it. She seemed terrifyingly competent, really.

Now that his hands were relieved of the jelly, he found he didn't know what to do with them. He shoved them in his trouser pockets, realized that made him look like a fool, and ended up merely stuffing them into the crooks of his elbows.

"I'm afraid Susanna found the boys to be too much and has had to take herself off to the shops. I shall be happy to tell her you called for her."

"Oh, I didn't call for her," he said, and then realized he sounded rude. "That is, I called to see your father. I need his advice about the estate."

The mask of haughty coldness descended again. Or perhaps it was more like distrust. She must know he was here to assess the mental state of her father and meant to turf him out as his aunt had commanded. He resisted the urge to hang his head and scuff a toe like a schoolboy.

"Certainly," she said, looking as though she was well aware that he didn't know a hoe from a hacksaw. "He will be delighted to talk with you about your estate. He's always loved Littleton Park. You have such a lovely prospect from the south windows and the low-lying land by the river has such promise."

He nodded vigorously so she wouldn't know he hadn't a clue what she was going on about.

"Lord Harrow—the former Lord Harrow—was one of my father's closest friends. He would dandle me on his knee while they discussed the improvements. When I was a child, I mean, of course."

Dandling the starchy Miss Faraday on one's knee would be an interesting prospect indeed. He wasn't certain he even wanted to envision it.

"Come," she said, the defiant tilt to her chin belying the polite invitation, "let's go to Papa's study. I'm certain he won't mind the fact that you dropped in uninvited."

Jack considered himself an expert on feminine snubs. After all, he'd been snubbed by some of the most elite hostesses in the kingdom. Clever women, beautiful women, rich women, well-born women— he'd had the condescending stare from any number of them. But never from a plain little nobody like Miss Faraday. Embarrassed annoyance rose within him. By Jove, he was going to enjoy giving her and her proud father their congee.

He followed her down the narrow hall lined with

grand views of estates. By jingo, but the man had improved every well-known estate in three counties. He was pleased to note he'd been to hunting outings and house parties at most of them. There. Just let Miss Poor-and-Proud look down her nose at him.

She condescended to speak to him at last. "Are you enjoying your time at Littleton Park?"

Now was the time to crush her with a thin smile and a wittily cutting remark. Instead he felt like a tongue-tied adolescent. "Suppose so," he heard himself say like a fool. "It's a bit grim here. It would be a bit of fun if we could have a Christmas ball."

How stupid. The sour creature already thought him a frivolous dandy. Where had the idea of a Christmas ball come from? He detested balls. He reminded himself that he didn't give a rap what she thought, and he would have a damned Christmas ball if it suited him to do so.

"How pleasant," she said, as though she would far rather spend an evening jabbing herself with an oyster fork. "Susanna would enjoy that."

The study was as blazing hot as the rest of the house was cold. All the oxygen seemed to have boiled away in the tropical heat. At the far end of the room, so close to the grate that it was a wonder the paper-thin man didn't go up in flames, was Mr. Faraday. He sat in an old bath chair, his lower limbs swathed in a smother of blankets, his long, veined hand twitching restlessly in his lap. At the wheels of his chair were two young boys amusing themselves by setting fibers from the carpet afire with a red-hot poker.

The man looked up and smiled calmly. "I predicted it would snow," he said. "And it has begun just now."

Miss Faraday swooped down to chastise her nephews.

Jack went over to the wheeled chair. "So it has, sir. My aunt will have to order the sleds out at last." He took the man's hand and shook it. "I'm Jack Harrow."

He really wished he didn't have to do this. How unfair of his uncle to leave him with this bumble broth.

Despite the feel of his frail bones when Jack took his hand, Faraday seemed lucid enough. Perhaps it was best to forget the entire thing and go home. After all, he reminded himself, it was his own estate now. If he wished to employ a man who enjoyed sitting in a bath chair in a room hot enough to poach one's brains, so be it.

Behind him he could hear the two boys obediently putting the poker back in the stand and going to sit stiffly in the windowseat. Obviously, Miss Faraday could take the joy out of anyone's day.

"Jack Harrow," the man repeated. "Beauford Harrow's nephew."

Indeed, sir." See, there was nothing wrong with Faraday. As much as Jack would like to see the man's daughter humbly pleading with him for the salvation of their livelihood, he could instead merely go home and have his dinner in peace.

"Tell Harrow to come and visit me," Faraday said. "Haven't seen him since I've been laid up."

He heard a crash as Miss Faraday dropped a shovel full of coals onto the inferno. She slipped over to her father, adjusting his rugs and moving him closer to the kiln-like heat of the fire.

"You know Viscount Beauford Harrow died last year, Papa," she said gently. "This is his heir, the new viscount." She smoothed her father's hair, the expression on her face quite different from the one she wore when she looked at Town dandies who had the temerity to inherit a grand agricultural estate.

"Harrow's heir," Faraday said, still with calm, unruffled pleasantness. "Yes, yes, I've heard about you. Harrow said you were a good-for-nothing rapscallion without a rational thought in your head."

"So I've been told, sir," he replied, shooting Miss Faraday a glance. Her straight brows rose in an expression of defiance. If he'd hoped she would be embarrassed at her own rudeness, or, perish the thought, defend him to her father, he was obviously wrong. She was a judgmental Greek goddess, an Amazon warrior woman, a shrew of Shakespearean proportions. All those wretched things one suffered through in school and never expected to meet.

He reminded himself that he was the one who held the power.

"Never do, never do," her father continued mildly. "Tell Harrow that that heir of his must be sent to me and I'll train him. Knock some sense into that wooden head. Give him a good grounding in agricultural principles."

"That's why I'm here, sir." Good God, he really hadn't meant to say that. The last thing he wanted was some kind of farming lessons. Fortunately, the man had turned his attention to the window and seemed to have lost interest.

No, better come clean and tell everyone exactly what he intended to do. There was no way this man was capable of acting in his former capacity. "What I meant to say was, I need to learn a bit about the estate." Jack cleared his throat. "Thought I'd ask your advice on hiring a new estate manager."

Mr. Faraday appeared not to have heard him, but continued to stare outside at the tiny flakes that were starting to weave their way toward the ground. His daughter, however, drew herself up to her full, skinny height and looked down her nose at him. Fortunately, he was taller than she and the effect was only a rather unattractive squint.

"But my father is the dowager Lady Harrow's agricultural consultant, Lord Harrow. He has been for years." She looked as though she would like to pull a thunderbolt out of that nightmare of a gown and strike him down.

"I thought—"

"You thought to replace him."

"No—that is, I—" He felt the schoolboy wiggles creeping over him again.

Miss Faraday's lips were pressed thin and her chin was held so high she had to half-close her eyes to glare at him from under her lashes. "My father has nearly fully recovered from his illness," she said. "He is out of mourning. There is no reason he cannot resume his duties. The estate has improved in productivity tenfold since he began his work here. You can have no reason for wishing to replace him."

Good Lord, but it was hot in here. Jack could feel his shirtpoints wilting. Beads of perspiration crept down his ribs, tickling him. This was difficult enough without feeling that any moment one might topple over from the heat.

He looked from Miss Faraday's tight face to her father's blank one. For a moment, he considered asking her to grant him a moment of privacy to explain that there was no use pretending. They could drop the drawing room manners and have a frank, rational, man-to-man talk. She would realize that it was obvious her father could no longer continue to manage the estate.

He then realized that she was not a man, he could not be frank, and she could not be rational.

He blotted his forehead with his handkerchief and then turned to Mr. Faraday. "Sir," he said politely, "what do you wish?"

Faraday looked at him, then went back to gazing out the window as though he hadn't heard.

"Sir," he repeated, louder.

"Papa, do you wish to continue managing the estate?" Miss Faraday asked, making sure her father was looking at her. It was obvious what she thought the correct answer was.

To Jack's surprise, the man gave an impatient sigh. "Tell Beauford here I'm too tired to ride out. You ride out with him, Olivia. Show him the drainage system in the south pasture and tell him we could do something like it with the lowlands below it."

He exchanged a glance with Miss Faraday. His faint shake of the head was met with an expression of violent disagreement.

He blew out his breath. "Excuse me for a moment, Mr. Faraday. May I have a word with your daughter?"

"Tell him yes, Olivia," her father muttered. "You're not likely to have another offer."

This time Miss Faraday did not meet his eyes, but she duly rose and crossed the room with him.

He noticed that the little boys on the windowseat had found a small rip in the cushion and were now engaged in pulling out the stuffing. They froze when they saw his glance, their eyes darting to their formidable aunt, but he said nothing. It gave him a small twang of pleasure to think of her annoyance when she discovered them.

"He wishes to continue managing the estate," she said.

"He said nothing but nonsense."

He saw an angry flush rise up her neck in a blotchy pattern. He felt a sudden sympathetic urge to take her hand and explain that it was not a personal attack; he himself said nothing but nonsense on frequent occasions. He felt like telling her he found it rather endearing how she protected her father. Rather like a mother bear who would cheerfully rip him limb from limb if she felt threatened.

Miss Faraday, her impassive face unable to contain her raw disgust, looked able to do just that.

The sitting-room door opened to let in a life-giving breath of cold air from the hallway. Susanna Clarke entered, in a lavender confection of a walking gown. At that moment, he could have thrown himself at her feet.

"Olivia," Mrs. Clarke was saying, "you haven't a single pretty thing in your clothespress for me to borrow."

She saw him and her expression lit up in the first smile he'd seen since he entered this house. "Why, Lord Harrow! How kind of you to call on us. I'm so sorry I wasn't at home to receive you." She fluttered over to him and placed her hands in his. "You're a naughty thing not to warn us that you might call. Olivia, I do hope you ordered something decent from the baker. I shall be mortified if we have to serve Lord Harrow some of those teacakes Molly made yesterday. They were really quite coarse."

"Mummy, I want an ice!"

"I want plums! You promised us plums if we were good!"

"Boys, honestly, give me a moment's peace. I want to talk to our visitor. Lord Harrow, did you meet my sons?"

Mrs. Clarke stretched out a hand to them and they obediently came to her side and offered twin bobs, meant to resemble bows. Jack admired them appropriately, glad to at least be back on ground upon which he was familiar.

He could feel Miss Faraday looming in the background, a disapproving specter.

"Will you stay for luncheon, Lord Harrow?" Mrs. Clarke asked. She attempted to wedge herself subtly between her darlings as their pinching and prodding devolved into something that looked likely to end in tears.

Luncheon with the Faradays? The arsenic with which Miss Faraday would doubtless season his food might be welcome. He shot that lady a glance, but she had picked up some mending and was virtuously sewing away as though her life depended upon it.

"I'm afraid I cannot trespass on your hospitality any longer," he said. "I am expected back at Littleton Park. I am sorry that you were not here when I called. However, your sister made me feel most welcome."

He shot Miss Gorgon a look to emphasize the sarcastic barb, but she appeared to have gone quite deaf.

"I was just going to walk to Littleton Park," Mrs. Clarke exclaimed, as though this was a truly remarkable coincidence. "I wanted to ask your housekeeper for a recipe for wassail. Did you know my sister doesn't have one? Nor one for Christmas pudding. Can you imagine being this close to Christmas and not having made a single preparation?" She gave a bright laugh. "La, I believe I shall have to take all the Christmas preparation upon myself this year." She gave her sister an arch smile that Miss Faraday ignored. "Since my sister seems to have no Christmas spirit at all."

"That," he said with the dignity and chill he hoped was worthy of a viscount, "I'm afraid I find quite easy to believe."

Five

"There you are!" Susanna exclaimed, coming into the kitchen where Olivia was trying to calculate how to stretch a pound of mutton to feed six mouths. "I knew I should find you here. I went into your room when I got up to see if I could borrow this cherry paisley shawl of yours but you weren't there." She settled the shawl around her shoulders and smiled. "You don't mind, do you, Olivia dearest?"

Olivia looked up from her list. "No, I don't mind." She drew a breath and decided that now was the time to settle a few things. "Susanna, you simply cannot lie abed until noon every day."

Her sister took up the elegant watch pinned to her bodice. "Is it really that late?"

"Nearly one. I realize you're in mourning and that you've had a tiring journey, but I truly do need your help."

Susanna gave her an apologetic smile. "I'm so sorry, dearest. I know I'm a terrible burden. I do try to keep the boys in line, you know. I suppose we'll have to hire a tutor for them, or at least someone to mind them. They so give me the headache." She wandered further into the kitchen, opening tins and peeking into canisters.

Olivia resisted the urge to snap that there was no way

in heaven they could afford a tutor for her nephews. Susanna wasn't saying it to be cruel; she simply had no idea of their current situation.

"I don't know why you persist in acting as though we haven't any money," Susanna said, evidently reading her sister's expression. "Papa says he has plenty of savings."

Olivia threw up her hands. "There isn't any savings. There was, but it's gone now. He just doesn't remember." If only Papa could take up his consulting again. She stifled that familiar refrain.

The new Lord Harrow couldn't see beyond his handsome nose. He wasn't likely to want to keep on an expensive gentleman agricultural consultant when he could hire an ordinary estate manager. Even without the way Papa acted.

Susanna found one of the teacakes she had maligned yesterday and dissected out a small piece. "What do you think of Lord Harrow?" she asked suddenly, as though her own thoughts had drifted in that direction as well.

Olivia turned back to her menu. "I don't know what to think," she said cautiously. "I hardly know him."

Susanna made a lascivious face over her mouthful of cake, swallowed, and then laughed. "You have eyes in your head. Don't be so missish. Is he not the most handsome creature you've seen in an age?"

That was not saying much. Olivia couldn't recall the last time she'd seen a man besides her father, Willard the butcher, or the detestable Reverend Eggart. "He is well-favored, yes."

"And wealthy. And titled."

And he might be persuaded to take Susanna and the boys off her hands, a wicked voice in Olivia's head added.

No, even Susanna didn't deserve a man without a

thought to call his own. She tapped her pencil impatiently against the scrap of paper she was using for her list. "But is he good?" she asked. "Is he kind?"

Her sister looked at her as though she were an imbecile. "Good? Kind? I don't know."

Perhaps she *was* an imbecile. After all, they claimed to be the daughters of a gentleman. Ladies of breeding married for practical, dynastic reasons. Ladies without money married for practical, financial reasons. Love matches were for actresses and farmers' daughters.

Still, perhaps it was possible for Susanna. She smiled. "I would not have Lord Harrow as my brother-in-law if he were not good and kind."

Brother-in-law. How humorous that would be. The man was a rattle if she ever saw one. Susanna would have him wrapped around her finger. Olivia wondered, for a flicker of a second, what it would be like to have a man wound around one's finger. To have a man who doted upon her. Who looked at her with an expression of devotion. Who loved her.

She straightened her shoulders and raised her chin. It would not be a man like Lord Harrow.

Susanna laughed. Not the pretty laugh she saved for a drawing room full of men, but a genuine, voluptuous laugh, complete with a snort at the end. "Brother-in-law! Lud, Olivia, how provincial you sound! Marriage! I ask if you think a man is handsome and you think I'm considering marriage. I only meant for a flirtation, my dear."

Olivia pretended to scribble a few more notes on her menu. Of course she was being provincial. "We can't afford a flirtation."

Her sister rolled her eyes. "I don't mean, of course, that I would not marry again. After all, being a widow is positively dismal. But, if we are to be frank, I married up in the world, and I am still young enough and pretty enough to aspire even higher this time. Higher than a viscount, anyway." Susanna saw her sister's look of shock and shrugged. "You needn't look so horrified, Olivia. I have a great aversion to being poor. Particularly if our circumstances are as dire as you seem to think. I have every intention of marrying someone with more money than even the handsome Lord Harrow."

Olivia tried to turn her mind back to mutton. It would be right to assure Susanna that she could marry where her heart took her. However, instead of feeling alarmed at her sister's announcement, she selfishly felt relief. Perhaps Susanna would marry for money. And perhaps it wouldn't have to be Lord Harrow.

Molly came in, her cap askew as usual. "Lord Harrow to see you, miss," she said breathlessly. "He said you were to show him the lower south field."

"Me?" Olivia exclaimed, indicating herself with a bewildered expression. She looked to her sister. "Not Susanna?"

Her sister patted the crumbs from her mouth with a tea towel. "Oh, I meant to tell you, darling. I had a little chat with Harrow yesterday when we took our walk to Littleton Park. He admitted that due to Papa's . . . condition, he was not certain that Papa could continue in his capacity as agricultural advisor. Now, stop making that face, Olivia. It will give you very ugly wrinkles when you are older. Honestly, my dear, I've always defended you when people called you a termagant, but I'm beginning to feel they were right. You really did frighten poor Lord Harrow."

"Frighten?" she said scornfully. What a hen-witted man he must be.

"Well, I think he might have been funning."

Olivia rolled her eyes. After all the work she did, after all she sacrificed for her family, people called her names? She felt anger and shame warring painfully in her chest. Perhaps she had been rather short with people in the village. She'd been absorbed with their troubles, distracted. She'd been positively rude to Reverend Eggart, though he deserved it. And to Lord Harrow as well. Though he deserved it more.

"I told him that he shouldn't make a decision without seeing Papa's work," Susanna went on. "I said you would show it to him."

"*I* would show it to him?" she echoed.

Her sister's delicate eyebrows arched in surprise. "Who else? Papa is too ill, and I don't know what's been done. Believe me, I would do it if I thought I could. *I* would make use of my time alone with the man. But you know all about Papa's improvements. You can show Harrow, and he'll know that Papa is indispensable. He promised me he wouldn't make a decision about hiring a new estate manager until after Christmas."

Olivia cringed. How stupid she'd been. She'd been a harpy, and worse, she'd let her prejudices blind her to practicalities. Susanna's idea was an excellent one. She could show Harrow Papa's work and then he would give up the idea of hiring someone else. Actually, even Papa himself had suggested she show Harrow the estate.

And surely she could be pleasant and charming. It wasn't as though she'd never had a beau before. Though the lecherous Reverend Eggart was hardly a man who would encourage one to cultivate charm. But she could be charming. Surely.

Susanna pulled the cherry paisley shawl closer over her elegant shoulders. "Lud, but you keep the house cold," she said mildly. "Now run along, sweet, viscounts don't like to be kept waiting. Though you should run a comb through your hair before you do. You look like you've been tearing at it like a madwoman."

She felt like a madwoman. But Susanna was right. Showing Harrow Papa's work was the only thing that could save them.

"Oh, and Olivia," her sister called after her, "tell him I'd be happy to go driving with him afterwards. I may not want to marry him, but there isn't any harm in keeping him just in case, don't you think?"

Olivia gave her sister an affectionate scowl and went to go and find a comb.

Six

Olivia came downstairs a few minutes later, her face washed, hair tidied, and stomach in knots. What did she know about her father's work? How could she show it off to best advantage? And as for an afternoon of being pleasant to a man she patently despised . . . For a moment she wished for Susanna's easy charm.

She made a quick detour into the sunny study where her father sat in his chair while her nephews amused themselves by drawing in one of his architecture books. The girl Susanna had brought with her from London had lasted all of two days in the country. The last straw had been the twins' attempt to put her in a sack to boil her like a Christmas pudding. She'd fled on the next mail coach.

Since then, the boys had been left very much to their own madcap devices. At a look from Olivia they scampered away, hooting like wild animals.

"Papa," she said, going to his chair, "Lord Harrow is here. I'm going to ride out with him to see the south pasture. What shall I tell him?"

To her relief, he looked up and smiled. "The south pasture. I worked on that two years ago. We put in French drains in the lane since it kept washing away and then built up the corner of the field to keep things from getting too boggy. I had them put in that row of poplars as well."

Olivia looked over her shoulder to see Molly ushering Lord Harrow into the room. Good. He would see very well that her father was not feebleminded. Soon Papa would be back on his feet and everything would be just as it had been.

She watched Harrow as he conversed easily with her father. How relaxed the viscount looked. And, of course, he was shockingly handsome in his dark gray tailored coat and riding breeches. With his highly polished boots and carefully but casually brushed hair, he had transformed himself from the dandyish town buck into the elegant country gentleman.

He laughed at something her father said, and leaned closer over the man to respond. How did he manage to seem so at ease with people? She envied his temperament, which seemed unflappably pleasant. But then, she reminded herself, it would be easy to be pleasant if one had more money than responsibilities.

At last Harrow turned to her and offered her his arm. "We should start out soon, I believe. The weather is fine now, but isn't likely to last all day. Your groom is waiting to accompany us."

Dear Willard, transforming himself from butler to gardener to groom according to their needs. She was grateful Harrow didn't know the whole of their circumstances.

She walked outside with Lord Harrow. It was odd being led along, as though she were an animal. As though she were delicate. But she reminded herself that this must be done, and be done graciously.

By the mounting block stood the family horse. Awkward, lumbering Gerald was the last relic from their splendid stables. And poor, blind old Trueheart was hobbling along behind the animal as though she expected to go along on the adventure.

It was hopeless to think a sporting man like Harrow would fail to notice the state of their stable.

"I'm afraid I'm a poor substitute for my father," she said, allowing Willard to help her into the saddle. "I'm sure in a few weeks he'll be able to show you the grounds himself."

"That horse is too big for you," Harrow said bluntly. "Would suit a man better." He looked the animal over with an expert eye. "You might find a lady's mount more comfortable. My aunt has a lovely mare, and since she doesn't ride, the animal is as plump and indolent as Lady Hamilton. I'll bring her over for you tomorrow."

Olivia wanted to object to his high-handed assumption that he knew what was best for her. But she didn't particularly wish to admit that they only had one horse, and it was indeed too large for her.

She forced the kind of smile she thought Susanna would use. "Thank you. That would be very kind."

To her surprise, he went a bit red in the face and then managed a boyish smile of his own. Harrow was always smiling, always laughing, but this one was different. It made him look quite appealing. Not at all like a viscount.

She must have dropped back into her usual expression, for his smile quickly faded. She swallowed, feeling suddenly awkward. How had she managed to survive a whole Season of this kind of banality?

Pleasant, empty conversation didn't suit her. No wonder she hadn't taken.

She cleared her throat. "Shall we ride out to the south pasture? My father thought the French drains there would interest you."

He looked anything but interested, but obediently

matched his horse's stride with hers and followed her down the lane. The silence became a rather long one. She wished, unaccountably, that she'd had Molly redo her hair. She could feel the cold, damp air pulling at flyaway strands beneath her riding hat. It was the same one she'd bought for her Season, so long ago. Likely a man of fashion like Harrow could tell to the minute exactly how old it was.

"Do you hunt, Miss Faraday?" he asked suddenly.

"No, I'm afraid I don't." Her father had, back in the day. But now, of course, both health and finances prevented it.

"No? Do you enjoy driving?"

"We haven't a carriage."

"Oh. How unfortunate. Perhaps you like to play card games. Whist?"

"I don't gamble, Lord Harrow," she said repressively. One caught more flies with honey than with vinegar, she reminded herself.

"I like to read," she volunteered. It was true enough, though she couldn't recall the last time she'd read for pleasure. Reading tradesman's bills didn't really count as reading.

"Oh," he said. There was a pause while he obviously groped for something to say. Not a great reader, she surmised. "I like the theatre," he said instead.

"I like the theatre, too." She beamed at him. There. They had something in common. Good Lord, but the south pasture was very far away today. She would have liked to launch into a comfortable discussion of plays, but she hadn't been to one in years. "I saw *The House in Essex* when I was in London last," she heard herself blurt. "Though that was over two years ago now."

To her surprise he looked uncomfortable. "I saw that,

too. With my sister and my fiancée." He looked at her and made a face of distaste. "I suppose you heard about that."

Frederica had mentioned something of a botched engagement. So it was true. She wondered briefly what kind of a woman would wish to marry Viscount Harrow. Certainly someone fashionable, someone with entree to the kinds of parties she herself had never been invited to attend. "I hear very little of town gossip here," she replied.

"She called it off," he said with a shrug. "Said we didn't suit. Which we didn't."

She looked at him. It was hard to tell if he was flushed or if it was merely the cold. For a moment she felt irrationally insulted on Harrow's behalf. Didn't suit, indeed. How cruel! His former fiancée must have been a very cold kind of woman.

She tried to imagine the kind of woman who would call off an engagement to a tall, handsome man with an easy laugh and pleasant ways.

Most women in London would fling themselves at him. The marriage mart would deem him charming, good-looking, and well-bred. Which was all anyone could ask for. With the exception of herself, of course.

She wanted to ask Harrow what the woman had been like. Was she beautiful? Clever? Did she love someone else? She wanted to know if he had been hurt or merely relieved, as he pretended. But those were not the kind of questions strangers asked each other.

She looked behind her to see if Willard was following. Poor man, he'd been forced to borrow one of Reverend Eggart's old nags for the occasion. She found herself wishing he didn't keep such a respectful distance. Though it was painfully obvious Willard was a rather makeshift groom, he knew everything about the estate. His presence might keep the conversation from vacillating between too personal and nonexistent.

Lord Harrow drew a breath as though he'd only now thought of a way to break the silence. "I hope you and your sisters will attend the Yule ball my aunt is hosting."

"A ball?" she echoed. How long had it been since she'd attended a ball? Since her Season, perhaps. The notion was appealing, though not practical, she quickly reminded herself.

"We are only recently out of mourning for my brother. And of course my sister Susanna is only just in half-mourning."

She saw again that easy smile. For some reason it made her frown. She didn't like the feeling it gave her in her palms and her stomach.

"Oh, don't scowl at me. It terrifies me," he said, with a grin calculated to infuriate her. "Do say you will consider it. I hate balls, myself. But I thought it would relieve some of the tedium of the country."

He saw her bristle and gave a helpless shrug. "It seems wrong not to celebrate Christmas. Everyone would have been highly disappointed if there wasn't a Yule ball. And now that my aunt has allowed herself to be talked into it, she has embarked on the plan like a military campaign. In my parents' home, a Christmas ball was the done thing."

She tried to imagine attending a Christmas ball, dancing the waltz in her twice-turned best gown, laughing and flirting with him, the dashing London beau. Ridiculous.

"Here is the south pasture," she said abruptly. "I'm sorry you never saw it before the improvements. It lies very low, as you can see, and used to slope more precipitously. It flooded so often as to be practically unusable. The fourth viscount, the one before your uncle, I mean, had it grown over and used for grouse cover. Your uncle had more practical views of land."

She saw him perk up at the mention of grouse. "Perhaps you would prefer that the land be let go again?" she asked. "I hope you will not. Your tenants have grown to depend on this land. To take their lease would be a hardship."

He shook his head quickly. "Of course not. We will continue to cultivate it."

We. The word unexpectedly warmed her. Perhaps that was a good sign.

"Let me show you how Papa solved the flooding problem. Can you take this fence?"

She needn't have asked. He had a splendid seat and took the fence in a neat, unshowy way that drew her reluctant admiration.

Olivia followed him. She was a fine rider, and she knew it. Was it vain of her to hope that he noticed? Perhaps she couldn't compete in a drawing room full of beauties, but she had other, more practical skills.

Then she remembered that she didn't give a fig what he thought.

She heard Willard swearing as his mount refused the hedge. Poor man, he looked miserable. The man hated riding, and it wasn't as though she needed an escort. Harrow was hardly likely to press her with unwanted attentions.

"The land was built up here," she said. "And Papa made a levee so that if the river should flood, the sheep would not have to be moved. Every other year we move the sheep and make hay."

He nodded his golden-brown head, a serious look on his face. He was doing a fair job of feigning interest.

Olivia drew in a breath of the winter air. It was a glorious day for riding—cold and misty, with the fresh scent of new snow. She couldn't recall the last time she'd ridden out merely for pleasure.

What would Harrow do for pleasure here? The villagers were a sober lot, hardly likely to provide him with the kind of drinking, gaming, and woman-filled entertainment he was doubtless used to in London.

To amuse himself, he wanted to hold a ball. A ball like those in London. She nearly laughed. Even if a fairy godmother produced someone to care for Papa, a glorious gown, and a golden coach, she would still be poor Miss Faraday, a jumped-up agriculturalist's daughter.

Assuming that she would even be invited.

She felt her spine stiffen. "I am glad you have decided to have a Yule ball, Lord Harrow, but I must warn you that you shall be setting a precedent. And if there is anything we're suspicious of in Littleton, it is a precedent. People here are hard-working. Even the best families think more about work than play. You may find that your ball is not well attended."

She hoped it wouldn't be. It would be satisfying on some level if his elegant ballroom was empty. But of course it wouldn't be.

He smiled at her, the smile she hated. The man was shallow as a puddle of water.

"Perhaps it is time they had a little fun," he said. "After all, it's Christmastime."

She squinted out over the fields. They were mostly fallow, cut down to stubble with every fourth field growing clover to replenish the land. Papa's predicted snow was still only occasional delicate flakes drifting down in erratic spirals. A silvery mist was creeping in between the poplars. The world she had grown to love in the five years they'd lived here now looked like an unfamiliar fairyland.

She shook off those romantic notions. The land was good. It was neat and cultivated, just as it should be. Her father's work of art. Even a man like Harrow must surely appreciate its solid perfection.

"You don't know the people of Littleton," she said. "When you are generous you will be regarded as frivolous and when you are kind you will be thought of as prying." She tried to sound arch, like Susanna, but didn't quite manage it.

His open expression twisted into something more amused. "Is that what *you* think, Miss Faraday?" He was laughing, but it was obvious he was waiting for an answer.

"I think you are a very lucky man," she replied at last.

"Lucky! I should say not!"

She rolled her eyes. "But of course. You come from a wealthy, respectable family. You had opportunities for education. And now you have inherited a viscountcy with a great deal of prosperous land."

He stared at her with a look of genuine horror. "But I didn't want that."

"It gave you a title and money. Even a man like you wants that."

To her extreme surprise, he heaved a sigh and shook his head. "You really do hate me." His green eyes gleamed with a rueful kind of humor. "Not that I blame you. I mean, I can name a dozen women who hate me. And, of course, hundreds more who aren't overfond of me, but mostly don't think about me at all. But you—" he gave an explosive laugh. "You really hate me."

"I don't," she said quickly. She didn't like him, it was

true. But it was primarily what he stood for that she disliked. Perhaps not he himself, exactly.

He threw back his head and gave a long, genuine laugh. The kind of laugh she'd never heard from a sober man before. It gave her the strange urge to laugh, too, but she did not. "And you are a terrible liar," he said. "Don't worry. I don't mind that you hate me. I don't blame you, really. I'm just surprised that you hate me already before I've really had the chance to muck anything up."

She pressed her lips together and said nothing. When he put it that way, she felt rather small. She'd judged him for what she thought him to be.

She reminded herself that he had every intention of removing her father from his employment.

"Papa cut down a row of hedges there to allow the sheep more room," she said, her voice curiously rushed. "The shade had kept anything from growing, and the land was always damp here so those areas never dried out."

"I never asked for this job, you know," he said cheerfully, as though she hadn't just changed the subject. "I think I'm only fit for the army, personally. Cannon fodder. But of course my father wouldn't let me go. My brother-in-law Lord Westhaven went, you know. Despite being the firstborn son. Quite the continental hero. But me, I was expected only to finish university, keep out of too much debt, marry some suitable creature, and generally stay out of everyone's way. Wasn't intending on being the hope of the Harrow line. My cousin was supposed to inherit."

"It seems as though nothing is as it should have been." She felt flushed and irritable. If he were thoughtless and stupid, she would have a much easier time hating him. Ugly would help, too.

They took the fence together this time and cantered across to the next set of fields. His animal was long-boned and spirited, but he rode it with utter confidence. There was nothing dandyish in the way he handled his cattle. They rode in silence for some time.

He turned to her again with his disarming smile. "Forgive me if I sound impertinent, Miss Faraday. But you seem like a rather bitter person."

"You do sound impertinent." She felt an unreasonable anger heat her face. Why should she care what he thought?

"Don't misunderstand me. I rather like it."

This further outrageousness somehow failed to mollify her. She turned her eyes ahead and pretended to be absorbed in the frosted landscape.

"Oh, botheration, I've put my foot in it. I always do, I'm afraid. I only mean that I find your candor, well, refreshing. Good Lord, you don't like that either. Bitter isn't necessarily a bad thing. I know several bitter people I rather like. That is, oh, dash it all—" he laughed ruefully. "I've made a hash of this entirely. I wasn't cut out for this sort of thing, as I'm sure it's rather obvious. Never had too much call to do the pretty."

She refrained from retorting that no one in their right mind would call his blunt conversation "doing the pretty."

"Well, I daresay we in the country don't stand on ceremony." She meant to say it lightly, but she could hear the crackle of sarcasm in her voice.

He thought them simpletons here in Littleton. He thought her a bitter spinster. He couldn't care less about her father's work and found this whole enterprise far too much work for his spongy little brain. Very well, she didn't give a rap.

"I didn't mean to hurt your feelings," he said suddenly. His voice was gentle, coaxing, like Christopher's was when he'd gone a step too far in teasing her.

She drew in a quick breath. The air was so cold it lanced into her head and made it ache. "Nonsense," she said. She paused for a fraction of a second, half hoping he would take back his words, soften them with the explanation that he'd said them wrong, that he was a hopeless idiot, and that there was nothing wrong with her.

"Well," she continued briskly when he didn't, "Father had the lane built up so it won't flood. It used to be that this way was inaccessible in the winter. Now we're able to sow winter crops and start the spring planting earlier."

For the rest of the afternoon Olivia kept the conversation entirely centered on estate matters. Susanna would have been disappointed at the level of charm she exhibited, but at least she managed to keep from regaling Harrow with candor he might have found a bit too refreshing.

Over the course of the afternoon she had to admit that he was a quick study. Despite his spongy brain. He started with no knowledge at all. For heaven's sake, the man didn't even know what season to plant flowers, not to mention grains or root crops. But he asked intelligent questions and listened to her lecture with rather gratifying attention.

She heard him give a low growl of irritation as they took the fence by the shearing barn. "Can't see that I'll ever understand this. When you explain it, I see why he's done things, but I never would have known what to do on my own."

"That's why you need my father," she quipped.

There was something ominous in the way he didn't answer. Instead he pulled up and dismounted and then went over to examine the drains at the bottom of the field.

She gave an impatient sigh and slid out of the saddle.

"I don't know why you're bothering with all this," she said, giving the skirts of her serviceable black habit a twitch and then stalking after him. "You don't care about it, and my father does. Just let him be, and then you can sit back and think about your balls and your high life in town."

Harrow bit his lip with an expression she could not read. His mouth was cut in a straight line above a chin that for the first time she saw was molded in the strong, square shape generally deemed stubborn. Her sister had called him handsome. And so he was. Right now, Harrow looked utterly, unapproachably so.

"Your father isn't well," he said quietly in a voice she'd not heard him use before. "As I've told you before, I'm prepared to do right by your family, but I must find an alternative solution for the estate."

"You told Susanna you wouldn't decide until after Christmas," she gasped, trailing after him. Was it possible he was so dense that he didn't see the things Papa had accomplished with Littleton Park?

To her surprise, he turned around and laid a hand gently on her shoulder. She wanted to jerk back, but somehow, under the weight of his palm, she was paralyzed.

"You don't see, do you?" His eyes were not laughing now, but were darkly troubled. "No. I see you don't. Well. It doesn't matter. I don't have a solution now anyway." There was a pause while he searched her face. "Come, let's talk of other things. This is all too much learning for a lackadaisical wastrel like me."

She felt for a moment as though she were suffocating. But somehow she didn't mind.

Harrow gave a laugh that sounded forced. "Tell me what my aunt should serve at the ball. She says she will have turtle soup, no matter how I tell her it's impossible to get this time of year." His hand dropped from her shoulder and the spell was broken.

She shook herself. Silly.

"I'm sure it's nothing to me. You'd do better to ask Susanna."

He paused, shading his eyes to the pale white sun and looking out over the pastureland on the other side of the river. "Likely so."

She followed him as he walked on. He took long strides across the crust of ice that covered the barren field. Each step crushed a confident footprint in its sparkling veneer.

"My sister is the perfect one to help you with your party," she said, slipping awkwardly across the furrows as she struggled to keep up with him. "She has been out in polite society. Her husband was a friend of the Prince. She is used to entertaining royalty. *She* isn't bitter," she added in a disgruntled mutter.

She nearly ran aground against his broad back when he stopped abruptly. "I really did hurt your feelings, didn't I?"

She looked up and found that he was staring down at her as though she were a curious sort of oddity. Once again, he wasn't laughing.

"Don't be ridiculous," she snapped. "It matters very little to me what you think of me."

He again smiled, but it didn't really reach his eyes this time. "Nor should it. Because I am only an irresponsible town dandy." There was wariness in his gaze.

As though he, too, wasn't certain what would happen in this forbidden, strictly personal territory.

"I don't—"

"No, you may be frank, Miss Faraday. It *is* what you think."

Her ears were burning with the cold and shame, and with anger as well. Why was she letting herself get drawn into this? In the air, the resentment fairly snapped between them. "Yes," she said, scowling. "There. We have it out plainly. I think you're a wastrel, and you think I'm a bitter old maid. Now shall we move on to a more productive avenue of conversation? The livestock, for instance? Papa has—"

His laugh shocked her. "Old? You malign me. I never said you were old."

She was caught off guard for a moment. "That's not my point, Lord Harrow. Now, sheep—"

"I think you're just the correct age."

Would the man never stop plaguing her? "Correct? For what? I'm no less than twenty!"

He looked somewhat surprised that she would question him. "For everything," he said simply at last. The laughter returned to his expression. "For enjoying yourself."

A sigh deflated her. He truly didn't comprehend.

To her surprise, he caught her chin in his hand and looked at her for a moment. The leather of his glove was warm and smooth against her cheek. She could smell the natural, rich scent of it. She wanted to slap him for his impertinence in judging her. She wanted to stomp away, remount her horse, and ride off home where she had better things to do than put up with this sort of treatment. Instead, she merely stood there, doltish, not resisting the warm fingers that held her.

"I'm trying, Miss Faraday." He raised his brows in an expression of sheepish hope and barely contained laughter. "I'm trying to learn to change."

Seven

The dowager Lady Harrow was not pleased. And when she was not pleased, she made damn well certain no one else was, either. The servants had been wearing tracks in the carpet scurrying to do her bidding. Every ten minutes another cart, rider, or runner was sent flying down the drive toward town on some dispatch or other. Once the dowager threw herself into the idea of the Yule ball, nothing by halves would do.

She'd spent the morning waging war in the kitchens; she'd then slashed her way through the conservatory, and had now settled down to plan a campaign of social domination that rivaled Napoleon's.

"No," she said, stabbing a short finger at an offensive list. "This will never do. We simply must have more than four musicians."

"I thought we'd decided upon only three, Aunt. I thought this was to be only a small gathering." Jack stretched out his aching feet toward the fire and looked longingly toward the decanter of port on the side table.

"Don't sprawl, boy. This isn't some gaming hell. Now, do go and make certain Billox got my order to get more wine. It would be shameful to run out, and we can always store it if we have too much."

"Aunt Alva, this isn't London. It would never do to

make our neighbors think we're showing off. Surely everyone will have a better time if we do something modest." He looked around the room. It was a good deal too late for that. Even this small drawing room had been decked within an inch of its life with evergreens and winter berries. Sugared fruits in silver cornucopias and small, wrought baskets dotted every surface. Even the candle stands on the side table had small, crystal icicles dripping from them. It was an orgy of holiday excess.

There were only a dozen or so families who could possibly attend. Perhaps a few more, if one included the tippling Reverend Eggart, his beautifully dowered sister, and the Faradays. He nearly laughed aloud. Miss Faraday would poker up at the crystal icicles, to be certain. It was just the kind of lavish display she despised most.

Had he really been so blockheaded as to suggest this ball? Who would possibly wish to come? Miss Faraday had been right. This would never go over with the sober people of Littleton. Instead of celebration they would see pretension. He would be off on the wrong foot from the beginning, just like he had been with little Miss Gorgon.

He'd been riding out to various parts of the estate for nearly two weeks now. She'd condescended to ride the horse he'd provided for her, but had evidently been determined to make up for that concession by being as crabbed as a cat in a hatbox.

But in Miss Faraday's tours, her father had earned a great deal of his respect. They'd tramped through miles of fields, examined the innards of pumps, admired the new poultry yard, and discussed the engineering of the river spillway, the placement of the smokehouses, and the anatomy of the buttery. And though Jack expressed his admiration of Mr. Faraday in the strongest possible terms, Miss Faraday still managed to look at him as though he were a slug in her teacup.

Frankly, he'd begun to enjoy it. It took so little to needle her, and she took such pains not to show it. But her face was an open book. The girl would have done better if she'd had a brother to taunt her. It would have made her a little less starchy, a little less shocked when he said something idiotic, as he always did. He thought of how he'd taunted Amelia and Miriam growing up. They'd learned to take it all in fun and give as good as they got. Miss Faraday, she only raised her chin and gave him that cool look of loathing. No sense of humor at all.

Then he recalled that Miss Faraday had had a brother after all. Dead now, poor devil. And even his presence hadn't been enough to take the razor edge off his poker-faced sister.

Perhaps he shouldn't be so critical. After all, she had enough on her mind. It was obvious that she was the only one in the family able to take care of things. And that was just the problem, wasn't it? She took everything a vast deal too seriously. Which was, perhaps, why he enjoyed infuriating her. Anything was better than the hunted look she often wore when she wasn't aware he was looking.

"Are you listening?"

"Yes, yes, of course, Aunt. The wine."

"I was talking about the Faraday girl."

He started, and felt an inexplicable heat rush into his face. "Indeed? I was just considering what we might do for her family."

"Do? So you think I *should* invite her?"

"Of course."

"But she is still in mourning for her husband. Not that she acts it, mind you."

He stared at his aunt. "Husband?"

The dowager waved her hand, nearly upsetting a pile of gilt-edged invitation cards. "Well, she isn't Faraday anymore. You know, the older sister. Clarke, I suppose her name is now."

"Yes," he said, recomposing himself. "Mrs. Clarke. Of course you should invite her sister, Miss Faraday, as well. I believe the youngest sister is not yet out."

This time it was his aunt's turn to look confused. "Now really, Jack. We can't just go inviting everyone. It will be a melee. And then the best people won't come. Mrs. Clarke married up, so there is no reason we shouldn't invite her. Her husband was in the Tenth Hussars. Dined often with the Prince, you know."

"Miss Faraday is quite genteel. You told me yourself that her father is one of the preeminent agriculturalists in England."

The dowager sat with her nose wrinkled for a long moment. "Yes, of course. But that's something different."

"Miss Faraday will come," he said firmly.

His aunt lifted her heavy shoulders and let them drop. "Well, we can invite her, but she likely won't attend. Mrs. Hepple, who is a good deal too frivolous and never discriminates as to who she invites, invited Miss Faraday to any number of dances for the young people last year and the girl has never accepted." The dowager turned back to her menus and appeared to consider the conversation closed.

Jack shrugged and went to the window. The heavy snowfall had put off this morning's lecture on farming improvements. He should feel like a boy with the day off school. Instead he felt rather annoyed to have his routine disturbed. Lord, but he was turning into an old man.

Yes, yes, back to the poxy Yule ball. Very well. It mattered little to him. If Miss Faraday wished to turn down invitations, if she wished to hole herself up and shoulder the burdens of the Faraday family alone, so be it. It was hardly his responsibility to be certain she was amused.

Mumbling about delivering the message to Billox, he turned and strode off toward the study. It was hard enough to get anything done here with every servant in the place racing up and down stairs, polishing and scrubbing as though their lives depended on it. He relayed Aunt Alva's orders, then shut the door to the study, leaned against its heavy oak panels, and indulged in a hearty laugh. Good God, he'd been the one who suggested his aunt have the party in the first place. He made his way over to the desk and opened the ledger. Getting too serious by half.

On the desk was the pile of letters he'd received this morning. He felt the laughter ebbing away. By jingo, why did life have to be so dashed difficult sometimes? Right now he'd give a monkey to be back in his former life, ordinary Mr. Harrow. Irresponsible, reprehensible, jilted, debt-ridden, jolly Mr. Harrow.

And, ironically, that former self would have stupidly given a monkey to be a respectable viscount with more money than he knew what to do with.

He picked up the first letter and broke the seal. It was from Hellion Harry, good old fellow. Wanted to know, without making mention of the fact that he'd helped Jack out of a sponging house some years ago, if Jack might find it possible to find a living for his brother. Jack sighed. He'd already gotten a half-dozen of these letters.

It was worse than being dunned by tradesmen. Far worse because these were lads he really owed something to. Of course, he owed the tradesmen something, too, but repaying someone to whom one owed a debt of honor, well, that was something altogether different.

Unfortunately for Hellion Harry and his brother, the living here was filled to bursting with the ample figure of Reverend Eggart. He perused the next letter. This was from his former future father-in-law, Mr. D'Ore. The man hoped sincerely that the fact that his daughter had jilted him would not prevent his lordship from continuing to order copious amounts of wine from his warehouse.

Jack smiled. That was easily accomplished. He liked the man's wine stock, and he was glad enough to be released from his entanglement with the chilly Miss D'Ore.

She and Miss Faraday would have been two peas in a pod. Both daughters of the fringe gentry; both humorless, prim creatures who could extinguish the joy in a room like a candle. He smiled. Though Miss D'Ore had set her cap at him, back in the day, Miss Faraday would never show such bad taste.

And she wasn't precisely humorless. She'd actually shown an edge of dry wit he found rather amusing. In the course of their rambles they'd developed a peculiar, curmudgeonly kind of friendship. He needled her, she snipped at him—but he could see that more often than not these days she was only rolling her eyes for show, and he was only irritating her for the pleasure of driving her to the point where she was so furious she had no choice but to laugh at herself.

He dragged himself back to the post.

The next two letters were begging loans; the following one was a short, scribbled note from Boxty Fuller in Rome, who refreshingly demanded nothing, and the one after that was an interesting one from Willy North. Willy had a cousin, due to inherit the grand sum of nothing, who had a yearning to become an estate manager. Couldn't Jack use a good man like that?

Jack sat down so quickly the leather chair made a comically rude noise. Now here was something he could do. After all, North had covered up a series of shocking escapades at Oxford, shared a dashing good tip about a horse at Ascot, and had let him kiss his very pretty sister in the garden at a masquerade ball. The least he could do was offer his cousin a position. A position he very much needed to fill.

It would mean breaking the news to Miss Faraday that her father was no longer capable of fulfilling the position. Of course, she must know already. She didn't want to know it, but he could see from the defiance with which she displayed her father's accomplishments on the estate that she must be aware that something was quite definitely wrong.

He would tell her. She was a rational woman. She would understand that it didn't have anything to do with the fact that he rather liked her father, and he certainly admired his work at Littleton Park. This was a responsible business decision.

There was a time he would have laughed good and hard at the idea of Jack Harrow making a business decision of any sort. But here was a chance to do right by the estate, do an old friend a favor, and end things tidily with the Faraday family.

After all, he was getting a bit too involved in their lives these days. Wasn't healthy.

While he cut his pen, he hummed a drinking song

from the days when he didn't have to get up at the crack of dawn and inspect sheep barns or rows of swedes. Yes, dispensing favors might be a rather jolly pastime.

He was just sanding the letter when there was a tap on the French doors. He started in surprise and then went over to see a smiling, freckled face pressed to the glass.

"Hello," he said, opening up the door and pretending that it was an everyday occurrence that a very young lady with snow liberally powdering her pelisse should come calling in this unorthodox manner. "I believe you are Miss Frederica."

She grinned. "You remembered! How clever you are. I was certain you wouldn't. Yes, I'm Frederica. I came to see how the preparations are going."

He stepped back a pace and let her breeze by him. To his added surprise she was trailed by two filthy ruffians who, beneath the mud and snow, he recognized as Mrs. Clarke's two darlings. "Preparations?" he echoed.

"For the ball. Yes, I know it isn't for another week. But it's all anyone is talking about. Particularly Susanna. In fact, she specifically asked me to ask you if you preferred blush or oyster."

"I'm sorry?" He resisted the urge to shove all three of them back out the French doors and pull the curtains closed.

"The colors," she clarified. "They're kind of a pinky and a whitish. I don't know. She just called them blush and oyster. She shouldn't be wearing anything but mourning, of course, but she says she'll lay off blacks for the occasion. Olivia's quite cross. I'll just tell Susanna blush, all right? It's vastly prettier—take my word for it."

Jack plucked one of the Clarke boys off the leather ottoman. "Excellent," he said. "I'm glad that's settled."

"Your aunt's Yule ball will be the event of the year." She raised her voice over the boy's insulted protest. "I'm not allowed to go, though." She gave a petulant scowl reminiscent of the twins'. "I'm not yet out, but it is very cruel of Papa not to let me attend. Especially when it is my one Christmas wish."

"Christmas wish," he echoed. Were all women like this? Slightly terrifying in their foreignness?

Miss Frederica looked at him with a somewhat pitying version of the slug look. "My sister has always said that everyone deserves a Christmas wish. And mine always comes true."

"Can't see why you'd want to go to a ball. All alike anyway," he muttered. He noted that the room had gone ominously quiet and looked around to see where the twins had gone.

"Susanna has put me in charge of her children," Frederica said, with a grown-up wave of her hand. "She is prone to the headache when they are around." She thought for a moment. "They came with a nursemaid, but she left. Which is good because Olivia said we couldn't afford her."

Olivia? Miss Faraday was named Olivia? He vaguely recalled that Mrs. Clarke had introduced her as such. What a spectacularly unsuitable name. Olivia was an exotic, sloe-eyed name. A name for a woman who might flash you a look across the rim of her wineglass, might throw out the occasional double entendre with an expression that dared you to acknowledge you understood. A woman who might promise you with the curve of her lips things that she never intended to follow through with.

It was not a name for Miss Faraday.

"Yes," he dragged himself back to the issue at hand. "She is always very busy. How is your father?"

Frederica twisted her mouth up in an expression of consideration. "Not very well, I think," she said at last. "He got lost on the way in to town yesterday. I suppose we should be glad he's up and walking. But it cannot be good that he doesn't know how to get to a place he's lived in all his life, is it?"

Jack felt a surge of relief to see the twins race by, engaged in a vigorous swordfight with a letter opener and a pair of scissors.

"And all week he's been going on and on about how someone has been stealing his shoes," the young girl continued. "Of course, I can't imagine why anyone would want to do that, particularly when his shoes are hardly anything fine. But he swore and ranted that they were being stolen. Of course, it turns out that he'd only put them in his desk. They'd knocked over an inkwell and got ink everywhere. Olivia was so cross."

No doubt she was, poor girl.

Frederica gave a philosophical shrug. For a moment she looked older than her years. "I feel sorriest for Olivia," she said. "She has to take care of him all the time. And sometimes he does go on and on about things no one understands. But she's always patient with him."

Jack considered suggesting that it might be best to separate the boys from the sharp objects they seemed determined to impale themselves upon. But by this point they were distracted by a stuffed pheasant his uncle had mounted on the study wall.

"Can you not afford to hire a nurse? And someone to care for these monkeys?"

Frederica shrugged. "No. I wish we could. We used to have any number of servants. Poor Susanna is in fits about it. She is used to having a large domestic staff when she was married. Captain Clarke was very rich. Or at least he spent a great deal of money. Susanna is always saying how hard it is to live now that she is widowed."

"We used to have Kitty to take care of us. And Nursey as well," one of the boys volunteered. Jack could never tell which of the rascals was which, but it was the one who had climbed up on a chair and was presently reaching for the pheasant's sharp beak. "Mama says that she will have to get married again very soon. She says you're a good catch."

Jack felt his face burn. It would be easier on everyone if he merely increased the annuity he intended to pay Mr. Faraday. Marriage, thank God, need never come into the question. For anyone.

The other boy ran over and attached himself to the leg of Jack's trousers. "I caught you!" he shouted triumphantly. "I caught you for Mama!"

Jack felt a wave of alarm. "So you did," he said, trying to sound cheerful. But I'm afraid your mama meant something entirely different."

He saw Frederica looking at him with an expression of open curiosity, so he composed his features. "Now perhaps you'd like to go down to the kitchen for some refreshment? I'm sure Cook has something you might like."

The boys shrilled their approval and went tumbling out of the room.

Frederica stayed where she was. "I was thinking," she said, looking at him with clear blue eyes that reminded him of Miss Faraday's. Only Frederica's lacked that metallic anger, that flash of fiery pain. Without those gorgon attributes, the youngest Faraday sister appeared rather ordinary.

"Excellent," he congratulated her. When she didn't

show signs of leaving, he motioned her out the door with a flip of his hands.

She didn't move. "I was thinking that if you didn't want to marry Susanna, you might consider marrying me."

He stared at her. "You?"

Her look of indignation was very like her sister's. "Well, why not?"

"Because you're far too young," he shot back, alarmed. "And I don't wish to marry at all."

To his annoyance, she nodded wisely. "Because of the jilt. I suspected as much. And I told Olivia so." She heaved a sigh worthy of an old woman. "But you must marry at some point. And you see, we Faraday girls must marry well."

"I don't wish to marry," he said again, feeling suddenly stubborn.

She stood up and shook out her skirts. "Well, that's why I thought you might wish to marry me. See, I don't particularly wish to marry, either, just yet. It used to be my Christmas wish that I marry you, but I've changed my mind. I think I would rather have my wish to be that I attend the Yule ball.

"Regardless, I thought we could plan to marry each other, and then, perhaps later, we might find that we didn't mind so much. In the meantime, you could take care of my family, and I would keep young ladies from throwing themselves at you."

"Tempting," he said dryly. "But no. You would be very sorry to be shackled to a rattle like me."

"But you are very rich," she countered with perfect gravity. "That would make up for a great deal."

He bit the inside of his cheeks to keep from smiling. "Perhaps. But I'm afraid at the moment I must still say no."

"I don't suppose you'd consider Olivia, then?"

He gave a rather ungenteel snort of laughter. "Do you think Miss Faraday would consider marriage to me?"

Frederica pondered this as though it had not been asked entirely in the interest of rhetorical sarcasm. "Likely not. She gets rather cross when anyone mentions you," she said. "And she's called you any number of names."

She considered the matter a little more. "But then again, the other day when Papa said you were a wastrel, she grew rather red and said quite sharply that you were making a great effort to learn. And she is quite particular about the cleaning and darning of the habit she wears when she rides out with you. And," the girl gave him an arch look, "I caught her trying her hair in a style we saw in the *Ackerman's* your aunt sent us."

Indeed, hardly the kind of evidence that would convince a judge. He gave an annoyed laugh. "I believe I'd rather drink hemlock wassail and sleep in a bed made of Christmas holly than marry your sister."

Frederica rolled her eyes and sighed. "She said very much the same thing."

He straightened abruptly. "She did?" He had the rather provocative mental image of himself and Miss Faraday in their holly-filled marriage bed.

"Well, she said something more along the lines of preferring to beg in the streets, but the sentiment was the same." The girl's eyes were sympathetic. "Which is why I thought you might consider marrying me. *I* would be kind to you."

He looked down at that grave little face, too young to care so much about so many things, and resisted the urge to wrap her in a fierce, brotherly embrace. "I know you would," he said with a smile. "But I want you to know—and you have my word on it—that you and your family will be taken care of. And you don't even have to marry me to be assured of it."

The tension between her brows did not relax. "Olivia said you would only pay us off and then throw us out."

He drew a quick breath. "I'll see that you're taken care of, Frederica. Don't ask for more than that."

A little taunting voice in the back of his brain reminded him that this was the way it was going to be from now on. People would expect him to take care of them. And more than that, they would want to be taken care of on their own terms. He shot a glance at the piles of letters on his desk and longed for the days when he was merely a demanding responsibility on someone else's pocketbook.

"Pardon me," Frederica said, with the vestige of a pout. "I didn't mean to make you angry."

He pulled a raveled plait, like he used to pull his sister Amelia's. "Steady Freddie," he teased. "It will all be all right. Now run along and see if your nephews have managed to set the kitchen afire yet."

Her good humor restored, the girl scampered after her charges.

Jack turned back to the desk. Marry one of the Faraday girls. Oh, his aunt would love that. Poor Frederica obviously hadn't grasped the subtleties of how these things worked. It was not a matter of choice or inclination. One merely looked critically at bloodlines and decided what alliances would produce the best offspring. Much like Mr. Faraday's sheep.

He smiled to himself. Yes, Olivia would appreciate that. While a dose of the fierce and independent Faraday clan might do the Harrow line some good, he doubted the resulting temperament would be worth the benefits.

Of course, thoughts of breeding led him on to different thoughts entirely.

He pushed the images from his head and tried to consider the matters at hand. Yes, there would have to be some changes in the Faraday household. He could offer them an annuity, but he could not let Faraday keep his position. He would break the news to Olivia immediately. This could not wait until after Christmas, though he'd said he would wait that long to make a decision. It was clear, no matter how she wished to deny it, that her father needed a nurse, not employment.

He opened up the books, settled his chair, stared at the accounts, mended his pen, readjusted the chair, gave the accounts another go, decided that the room was too dark and opened the curtains wider, then settled in the chair again. Olivia. What a name. He'd really thought of her as more of an Ellen. Or perhaps an Enid. Not an Olivia.

In the next room he could hear the servants laughing as they tacked greenery to the cornices and fashioned kissing boughs.

Sheep. He really must focus on sheep. Perhaps, if Miss Faraday had more help at home, she might be able to educate him as to why it was so dashed important to care about the lineage of his sheep.

And after all, there was no one in this godforsaken place who was half so much fun to infuriate as Miss Faraday. No doubt her lessons on sheep breeding would provide countless opportunities to make her so angry she'd burst out laughing.

He stared at the accounts for a few minutes longer. Then, with a sign of resignation, he slapped the book shut and went to ring the bellpull.

Eight

"You turned her off?" Lord Harrow stomped into the small drawing room without so much as a civil word of greeting. "I send you a nurse and you turn her away?"

Olivia looked up from the household accounts. "Lord Harrow," she said, pretending to be calmer than she felt. "An unexpected pleasure." After all, she'd expected he might barge in here when that woman reported back to him. She rose from her desk and resisted the urge to touch her hair to be certain she hadn't disarrayed it during her bookkeeping. The accounts these days were hardly in a state that would render one composed.

"I was trying to do something kind for you, Miss Faraday. I thought you might wish for some assistance with your father."

She drew herself up as coolly as she could, annoyed to find her heart pounding faster. "We do very well on our own, Lord Harrow. Though I do thank you for your generosity, I'm afraid it was a kindness we simply could not accept."

She watched him pace the room, huffing, evidently unable to join words together in his irritation.

She pressed back her own rising ill-temper. Of course she'd wanted to keep the woman. But just because he came here nearly every day to ride out on the estate didn't mean he could run tame here. And it certainly didn't mean he had the right to assess their household needs.

She set her hands on her hips, girding herself for battle. It was best to set things straight right away. Otherwise, he would only continue to meddle.

Harrow drew off his greatcoat and flung it into a chair. Apparently he felt the need to have it out, barefisted, as well. Perhaps she had been too sharp with the nurse. The woman probably exaggerated it out of all proportion when she reported back to her employer.

She should feel grateful for his generosity. But how could she when it was done in such a high-handed manner? The viscount knew everything she needed, and he was just going to take care of it with a snap of his aristocratic fingers?

"There is no need to be missish about all this," Harrow ground out. "It is not as though I sent you a lavish gift or something personal. Devil take it, I didn't even mean it as a present to you. It's for your family. This is practical." He stopped and pushed a finger in her face. "And you are forever accusing me of not being practical."

She stepped back slightly, unwilling to be intimidated by his height or his closeness. "What did you want, sir? Did you expect me to fall into curtseys and thank ye kindly, milord?"

To her surprise, he looked wounded. "I didn't do it to seem generous. I thought it would be something, well, something thoughtful." He made a frustrated gesture. "There is no pleasing you."

She did not explain that she did not wish to be pleased. And she particularly did not wish to be pleased by him. She did not want people's pity. She drew a breath and forced herself to be calm. Calmness was always more effective than passion.

"Your gesture was very kind," she said, attempting diplomacy. It *was* thoughtful. Perhaps that was why it made her so ashamed. Ashamed she'd been so bad-tempered, and more than that, ashamed she'd needed the help. It had been obvious to everyone, even to the rather unobservant Lord Harrow, that she was incapable of taking care of her family.

"You need a nurse," Harrow said with a shrug. At her expression, he rolled his eyes in disgust. "Olivia, don't poker up like that. Mrs. Smythies was recommended to me as a woman who knew nursing, but I don't care what you do with her. Have her take care of those twin imps. Have her help that poor, overworked maid of yours. You don't have to have her nurse your father. I just thought—"

Her name in his mouth sounded soothing, sensual. Rounded and voluptuous in a way she was not. She felt herself going hot with anger. "I did not give you leave to address me by my Christian name, Lord Harrow. Would you take such liberties with your social equal? Or do you think I'm someone below you, a servant perhaps?"

He made a gesture of finality and sighed. "As you well know, *Miss Faraday*," he hissed out her name dramatically, "I'm the kind of thickheaded fool who would call the queen by her Christian name, except that I'm rarely sober enough to recall it."

"Everyone calls the queen by her first name," she quipped.

He pretended to consider this for a moment. "I detest it when you make a good point," he said ruefully at last. "Quite takes the wind from my sails. What I should have said, of course, was that I don't think you're a servant, but that there are times when I think you're a fishwife."

She knew she was being teased, but she was not quite

ready to relinquish her annoyance. "Well, how would you feel if I called you Jack? Dropped all social niceties and slapped you on the back like one of your drinking cronies?" she asked. "That wouldn't please you, I know."

To her surprise he grew a bit red in the face. "Actually, it would please me enormously." He wandered to the window and looked out for a moment. "Perhaps not the slapping part. Might damage my coat. And I suspect you could hit dashed hard. But I wouldn't mind about the name thing."

She tried to imagine a situation in which it would be appropriate for her to do so. She felt her own face growing red as well. "Well, I won't."

He grinned. "I suspected as much. But perhaps we could choose another name I could go by."

"I have a few suggestions," she said dryly. She came up behind him, her hands on her hips.

"Perhaps His Most Eminent Cleverness."

"Perhaps Jack Dandy," she countered.

"Sweet Pea?"

He was distracting her from the point of the argument with his silliness, his usual tactic when they squabbled. Still, a giggle bubbled up. "Lord Cox-comb."

"Never. You do me discredit. Lord Bountiful, if you please." He gave a foppish bow.

She was laughing hysterically at this point. "Perhaps something manly. Harrow the Harvester."

"Jack, Subduer of the Bovine Hordes."

They were standing close together now, nearly bent over with mirth. He had jollied her out of her ill temper as usual, but somehow she couldn't resist him. "No, no, far too fierce."

"Little Luscious Lambikins?" he proposed.

"My Mangel-wurzel?"

"Precious?"

She could not breathe, she was laughing so hard. She put a hand to the stitch that was forming in her side and stood up, trying to catch a breath. "Darling?" she gasped.

He straightened, too, wiping his streaming eyes. "I think you would mind 'Jack' less," he said, sounding almost serious.

"Jack," she said softly, mostly just to hear how it felt to say it.

"That's much better." He was not laughing at all now, but he still stood very close. He bent his head, so that his mouth was but a breath from her own. "Olivia, I—"

Two familiar sets of footsteps came rumbling down the hallway. Olivia moved away from Harrow; she wrapped her arms around her waist, determined to forcibly control the torrent of emotions she did not wish to feel.

The twins entered the room at a run. Then, in a rather spectacular fit of flailing, George slipped on the rug and fell flat on his back. Teddy began hopping back and forth from one foot to the other, agitated by his brother's wails but determined to deliver his message.

"Aunt Olivia, Mama told us to come and find you to tell you that Grandpapa is driving her distracted. He's asking about the sheep and Mama doesn't know anything about any sheep."

Olivia set George back on his feet and patted him into some semblance of calm. "I'll be there in a moment." She shot a look at Lord Harrow. "Papa is concerned about next year's lambs," she informed him pointedly. "We should have begun the breeding several months ago. We shan't have any lambs this year if we wait."

He grew inexplicably flushed at this announcement. "Breeding," he echoed. "Sheep."

Good. Let him see that he needed Papa. She turned

her attention back to the boys and tried to calm the uncomfortable sensation that was bruising her own insides.

"Where is Frederica?" he demanded of the boys. "Shouldn't she be minding you?"

Lord, but the man was sounding more and more as though he thought he owned the place.

"Freddie is helping Mama with her gown for the ball," George informed him, still sniffling. "She is having a problem about ferns."

"What the devil?"

Susanna was supposed to be looking after Papa, not fussing about with her wardrobe. Olivia closed her eyes and drew a breath to calm herself. Obviously the strain was telling on her. One moment she felt like weeping, the next like laughing. And the next something entirely, humiliatingly unutterable.

"My sister cannot decide what color to wear to your aunt's Yule ball," she said. "We'd narrowed it down to oyster or blush, but now it appears that fern is back in the running." She stood to her feet. "I'm sorry, Lord Harrow. I'm afraid you've caught us at rather a bad time. Perhaps you could return—"

"Lord Harrow," Susanna swept into the room, all smiles. "I didn't know you had arrived." She swept him a graceful curtsey.

Olivia noted that for the moment her sister had opted for a stylish, rust-colored carriage dress trimmed with sable. Perhaps not strictly half-mourning, but very flattering indeed.

"You're early, you naughty man." Her sister stepped up to Harrow and pressed a long finger into his lapel. "And you're lucky I didn't make you wait for hours on end. It's shockingly impolite to make a lady rush." She looked up at him through her lashes.

"My apologies," Harrow returned, bowing. "I had some business to attend to first."

Olivia stood woodenly, feeling as though she were watching a play. The man she had just been laughing with and her flighty sister had just been transformed into elegant beings, their gracious manners decorated with the sparkle of flirtation.

"Are you going driving with Lord Harrow?" she heard herself say in a voice like a child wounded at being left behind. In an instant she was her fifteen-year-old self again—thin, plain, and awkward, and so terribly envious of her glamorous elder sister going off to London for her Season.

Susanna turned to her with a swish of sable. "Oh, I meant to tell you, dearest. In fact, I really thought I had. Perhaps I did. You've been very distracted lately. I know I certainly told you that I don't eat boiled eggs, and yet Molly brought them again this morning."

She gave a pretty little laugh. "Lord Harrow has been kind enough to offer to drive me to Bedford. You know Littleton has no shops of any consequence, and I simply must have a bit of lace for the carriage dress I intend to wear for the Yule log outing. Now, you needn't give me that look, Olivia. I am using my own money from my widow's pension. Surely you can't begrudge me that."

Olivia busied herself in brushing at the unidentified stains on George's coat. "Yule log outing?"

She saw Harrow's boots approach. "It's tomorrow," he said. "We're going to gather in the Yule log. I've invited my sister and her husband and, of course, my aunt has invited Lord and Lady Toby and Reverend Eggart and his sister. A small gathering, really." She heard his voice grow closer as he leaned down. "I hope you'll come, too."

Tomorrow? She'd thought she and Harrow were to go inspect the mill tomorrow. This had all been planned without her. "I cannot. I must—"

"That's why I hired Mrs. Smythies," he went on. "It was merely out of my own selfishness, you see. I wanted you to be there."

She continued straightening George's coat, while the boy attempted to evade her grasp.

"It's one afternoon, Miss Faraday," he said quietly. "Surely you can spare us one afternoon."

"Lord Harrow, here is Frederica," Susanna said cheerfully, sparing Olivia the necessity of making up the kind of frail excuse that would allow them to feel good about inviting her without actually having to insist that she come.

"I hope there is room for her in your carriage. Of course, you likely thought I would come with you to Bedford all on my own, but you cannot have thought me such a scatter-mannered thing." She laughed her beautiful society laugh. "I may be a widow, and this may be the furthest point on earth from London, but I still have my reputation to protect."

Lord Harrow bowed again. He gracefully concealed the chagrin he must doubtlessly be feeling. Why didn't Susanna go alone with him, make him fall wildly in love with her, and be done with it? It would be so much more efficient. And less painful for everyone.

How silly to have thought—

"I want to go into town," Teddy announced.

"Me, too! I want to go with Mama," his brother chimed in.

Her sister patted their heads with an indulgent look. "No, my sweetlings. I cannot take you with me. There isn't room for you in the carriage. But I shall bring you back a treat. Now you stay here with Auntie Olivia and be good."

"I'm tired of being good. I'm tired of staying in the house. I want to play outside." Teddy's voice was dangerously near a whine.

"You'll have to wait until Frederica gets back. I have to stay with Grandpapa," Olivia explained. "Perhaps you could ask him to read you a book."

The boys looked disgruntled. "Grandpapa shouts at us. He thinks we've come in to steal his shoes."

Olivia pretended she hadn't heard them. She could feel her face drawing up into the familiar tight-browed, thin-lipped expression.

"Please let me go with Susanna, Olivia," Frederica pleaded. "She said this outing was to be my special treat for taking care of the boys all week."

Olivia resisted the urge to clutch fistfuls of her silly new hairstyle. Of course it was unfair to expect Frederica to help with the boys all the time. She deserved more pleasure in her dreary life.

They couldn't go on like this without more help. She vowed to have a serious talk with her sister when she returned. Susanna, while she had begrudgingly taken over a portion of the running of the household, would have to take on more of the caring for her wild boys.

From her father's study at the back of the house, she heard his bell ring.

"Perhaps," Lord Harrow said quietly, "you and the boys could play in the snow outside of Mr. Faraday's window. Then you could let the boys play and still see if your father needed you."

It was a solution, she admitted ruefully. "Get your coats," she said to the boys. "But remember that we must stay by the window." She smiled at Harrow. "An excellent suggestion. Thank you, sir." Instead of sounding collected and grateful as Susanna would have, she heard her voice sound flat. Well, no matter.

"Now," the viscount continued, stepping closer, "I will not press you again, but I wish you would consider accepting the services of Mrs. Smythies."

Olivia did not like it when he used his persuasive voice. She had the mad feeling that she would do anything he asked.

"What?" demanded Susanna. Her hearing was apparently extremely acute. She gave a bright laugh. "Is Lord Harrow foisting his attentions on you, dearest? You must not take him too seriously. A green girl like you could get her heart broken, when it is well known about Town that Lord Harrow is a true care-for-nobody."

"It is a matter of the estate," Jack assured her with unmistakable coolness. Then he turned to Olivia. "I hope you will consider it, Miss Faraday. Consider Mrs. Smythies' services a gift of my aunt, if you cannot bear to accept them from me."

Olivia had spent many hours in Harrow's company with no more company than Willard. Why was it that now, in a room full of people, she should suddenly be put to the blush by the serious expression in his green eyes? "I will consider it," she mumbled.

Her father's bell rang again, this time impatiently.

"And the Yule log outing?" Harrow pressed. "I, we . . . we would very much like you to attend."

"No, really—"

"Just consider it."

She paused, arrested again by his expression. It was not pity, as she expected. It was not even kindness. She felt her throat tighten. "I'll consider it."

The bell jangled again, so Olivia made her way toward the door. Out the front windows she could see Harrow's coach and his footmen, dressed in splendid livery. They seemed ridiculously out of place in her ordinary life.

"Oh," Susanna cried out, pulling on her cloak, "silly me, I nearly forgot to ask you. Do you want anything from town?"

Olivia turned back from the door, unable to meet the eyes of the beautiful couple before her. "No," she assured her sister firmly. "I don't want anything at all."

Nine

Jack had found himself hoping that Miss Faraday would change her mind and attend the Yule log outing, but nonetheless, he was surprised when he looked absently from the upstairs window and saw her and her sister coming up the drive.

Mrs. Clarke was struggling along in lovely little shoes far more suited to the London pavement than any sort of country outing. Her sister wore unfashionably sensible half-boots and the old blue cloak she always wore.

They were a study in opposites, the Faraday sisters. Whereas Susanna was splendid in a mink-edged spencer, Olivia looked just as she always did—blue cloak, plain bonnet, drab gown. He thought of her trying to do her hair like the fashion plates. The idea made him smile. Though he had to admit, the new style of intricate braids twisted high on her head suited her delicately boned face better than the scraped-back knot she used to wear.

Actually, she had been looking rather prettier lately. Not that he had mentioned it. If he had, she likely would have lopped off that abundant honey-brown hair, donned the old bombazine bag of a gown, and painted her face blue just to spite him.

Oh, but yesterday had been a close run thing. Another moment and he would have kissed her. And then been swallowing his teeth after she landed him with a left hook.

What mad, self-destructive impulse had *that* sprung from?

He laughed quietly to himself as he went downstairs. Who said country life was dull? What with his constant spats with Olivia, advances from her sister, a ragtag troop of neighbors, and his aunt, who was growing alarmingly more enthusiastic about every aspect of the Christmas celebrations, the outing would be nearly as pleasant and convivial as a corn riot.

By the time he'd settled several last-minute preparations with the staff, more of the guests had arrived. Dash it all, but his aunt had done her research. She'd invited the cream of good society. The Yule ball would doubtless be attended by everyone in a twenty-mile radius who could reasonably be called gently bred. The Yule log sledding party, however, was made up of a select group.

The people rapidly filling up his aunt's drawing room were carefully matched in lineage and a perfect mix of ages and sexes. They all wore variations of the same fashionable country attire and they were all already partaking liberally of Cook's special spiced punch. It was all the tiresome things about London squashed into one small, overheated room.

He saw his aunt bearing down on him, her smile dangerously fixed and her knuckles white around her punch glass. His innocent confusion was replaced with dawning horror. The gathering was perfect but for one thing. One fly in the ointment. The Faradays.

"Jack," his aunt said with terrible cheer, "I hadn't realized you were intending to add guests to our little party."

He gave a sheepish shrug. "I met Mrs. Clarke and Miss Faraday yesterday, and thought I would invite them."

"How lovely," the dowager crooned, looking like she'd like to box his ears. "And after all, this is *your* party in *your* house. . . ."

"No, Aunt Alva, I—"

She pinched her lips together and tried to smile. "Of course, I can ask Lady Toby and Lady Ramsbottom to stay behind. The sleds will not fit everyone now."

Oh, he was in the suds now. He took a glass of punch from a passing footman and tipped it back. Out of the corner of his eye, he saw Olivia Faraday do the same. "Nonsense," he said. "Of course we will all go. It will be more cozy this way."

Mrs. Clarke chose this moment to punctuate her conversation with Lord Randolf with a loud shriek of laughter. Devil take it, he might as well have invited a pig to a christening. What had he been thinking?

The type of people he would invite to a sledding party would necessarily be gauche. They certainly wouldn't be the sober, upright kind of people a viscount *should* invite. Not that he would ever be able to figure out how he was meant to behave. He looked around the room, wondering what he had done to deserve this wretched inheritance.

In thinking it over, plenty.

Olivia had been buttonholed in a corner by Reverend Eggart. The man had breath that could fell an ox. Olivia was wearing her most unapproachable face, brows haughty and fixed, but the man was undeterred. Jack hoped the man wasn't foolish enough to renew his suit.

He noted that Olivia's discomfort showed only in the steady progress she was making through her second glass of punch.

Her sister let out another shriek of laughter and tried to drag Lord Randolf toward the kissing bough. The unimpressed gentleman was attempting to politely extricate himself. Why had he invited them?

Aunt Alva's lips thinned. "Well. We will have to do what we can. I suppose it's too late to change the guest list now. Really Jack, what were you thinking?"

She latched herself to his arm and took him around to introduce him to her guests. He smiled and nodded, acutely aware that he would not be able to recall a single thing about any of these people the moment he turned away. Dash it all, but he was not cut out for this country squire job. And who knew the wilds of Bedfordshire could produce so many blue-blooded bores?

He looked around to see how Olivia was faring. Was she hopelessly out of her element? Poor little gorgon. No doubt she would be feeling overwhelmed, and therefore irritable, at being faced with so many grand and aristocratic people. Just his luck when he had made so many ludicrous promises as to the fun to be had at this outing.

To his surprise, she had escaped Eggart's sermon, folded herself up at the corner of the sofa, and was conversing quite calmly with the ancient Lady Toby.

Of course Olivia could take care of herself. She was as inhumanly competent as an elegantly designed machine. Though there was beauty in function, perhaps. He had to admire that. The woman made it damned hard to feel needed, that was certain. But at least she could be counted on not to embarrass herself.

He saw his sister Amelia and her husband across the

room. They must have just driven in from Crownhaven. Thank God there was *someone* here who wasn't buttoned up to the chin and stuffed with sawdust.

His progress toward them was impeded when Mrs. Clarke attached herself to the arm not claimed by his aunt. "Lord Harrow," she exclaimed breathlessly, "what a charming party. I was just talking to Lord Pennyworth about it. Can you believe he and I never met in London? I've promised to show him all the sights there next Season."

She gave a pretty giggle and pressed herself closer to him. He felt his aunt's arm tighten into a claw on his other arm.

"We were just discussing how we shall divide ourselves into the sleds," Susanna Clarke said. "Do assure me you don't mean to separate the boys and the girls!"

After listening to it for two hours yesterday, the charm of Mrs. Clarke's laugh had well and truly worn off.

"I had intended—" his aunt began.

"We must make up a party of younger people and those of older people," young Pennyworth exclaimed. The young man glowed with puppy love, immune to his hostess's glare. "I say, it will be jolly fun altogether."

Jack detached himself, deciding now might be the appropriate time to check to be certain the servants loading the hampers and hot bricks into the sleds had everything they needed. And then perhaps to shut himself in the broom closet until this was all over. To his surprise, his sister followed him outside.

"How are you faring, Jack?" she asked, the laughter in her voice suggesting she knew very well that he was suffering a living hell.

"I'm being punished for all the times I teased you

when we were children," he said dolefully. "Aunt Alva—"

"Yes, yes," she interrupted, "Aunt Alva. But to be perfectly frank, Jack, badgering must suit you. You're looking very well."

He gave her a baleful glare.

"Indeed," she insisted, all innocence. "When I saw you last you were very thin, had been overindulging far too much, and were, of course, rather shockingly in debt."

"I've had this wholesome life thrust upon me," he grumbled. "I never wanted this title, this estate—"

Amelia gave him a cheeky smile. "It's good for you. And believe it or not, you're good for it. Aunt Alva says you ride out every day to learn more about the estate."

His collar inexplicably seemed to be constricting on him. "A man must learn something of his responsibilities."

He thought for a moment his sister would drop into fits from laughter. She recovered herself at last, gasping. "There is no sense in trying to pull the wool over my eyes. I've figured out the whole. And she's very pretty, too."

He drew himself up, shocked. "I have no idea what you're going on about." To his utter mortification he felt his ears growing hot. He hadn't blushed since he was a boy. He cleared his throat, affected by the tight cravat. "Now, where is that husband of yours? He's likely been trapped by Aunt Alva, wanting to hear about that child of yours. How is my nephew?"

Amelia's face lit up at the mention of her firstborn. "Oh, he's adorable, Jack. Just like his father. Why, just yesterday—" she propped her hand on her hip. "Now you are only trying to distract me. It's no use. We were speaking of the woman." She narrowed her eyes at him, the stern look at odds with her good-natured face. "I can't say that I wholeheartedly approve, but I must say she's a sight better than Miss D'Ore. At least she has some vivacity."

He marveled that his sister could have managed to plumb the depths of Miss Faraday's reserve in so short a time. Still, it was ridiculous. He might feel a slight partiality for the lady, primarily because she'd shown the good sense to despise him, and somehow his sister, who thought herself omniscient, had already planned the wedding.

He stood up straighter. "I assure you, Miss Faraday—" He stopped when he saw Amelia's eyebrows fairly fly off her forehead.

"Miss who? Faraday?"

They stared at each other for a moment.

"I thought Mrs. Clarke," she admitted at last, obviously entirely taken aback that she wasn't always correct. "She does seem rather more in your style." At his expression of horror, she elaborated. "She's beautiful, you can't deny. And she's lively, sophisticated—"

"Shallow, vain," he continued.

She raised a single brow. "That never bothered you before."

He resisted the urge to shove a handful of snow down his sister's back as he had found most effective when they were children. "People grow up," he said with great dignity. "Besides, Miss Faraday—" he halted. This was not where he wanted this conversation to go. "You must be chilled. We should go in and tell the others that the sleds are ready."

Amelia grabbed his sleeve. "Which one is Miss Faraday? Not that little mouse on the sofa! The one the

Reverend Eggart said was so unfriendly? Aha!" she crowed. "It *is* her! Well, if Eggart doesn't approve of her, then I most definitely do." She seemed to find this enormously amusing. "Oh, I was so wrong, but I was so right!"

He turned from her in embarrassed annoyance. "She isn't— You're imagining things, Millie. Must be the new motherhood."

"I knew you looked like a man in love, but I couldn't figure out who. I only knew Aunt Alva was cross. How famous! She'll lead you on a merry dance. Miss Faraday, I mean, not Aunt Alva. Though of course Aunt Alva will as well. Miss Faraday is as prim as Miss D'Ore, only brimful of virtue. Oh, Hunter will have such a laugh."

"Millie, you're being ridiculous. Your wits are addled. I am trying to better myself by learning more about the estate. Miss Faraday has been generous enough to help me. Neither she nor I find the experience particularly pleasant."

Amelia stared at him with a blank expression for a moment, and then her mouth sagged. "Oh, Jack, I'm sorry," she said, taking his arm. "Perhaps I am addled. I didn't mean to hurt your feelings. I can see that you take your duty seriously." The expression of contrition in her eyes turned suddenly to alarm. "Oh, Miss Faraday, I didn't see you."

Olivia smiled at them, her perpetual calm unruffled. But Jack knew she must have heard them. She was unreadable, as always. "Your aunt sent me to see if the sleds were ready," she said. "She's worried that if we don't set off soon, the guests will partake too liberally of her Christmas punch."

"Of course," Jack said quickly and far too jovially.

And then, because she stood there saying nothing, he repeated the phrase several more times, checking the bricks and rugs piled high in the sled.

Amelia took pity on them at last. "Miss Faraday, shall we go and get the others? Jack keeps uncovering the bricks so often, they'll lose all their heat. Though of course with the dowager Lady Harrow's punch, everyone may be warm enough."

His sister, when she put her mind to being charming, was impossible to resist. She linked her arm with Olivia's and led her off, prattling away as though they'd been friends from the schoolroom.

Jack watched the two women retreat back into the house. Had Olivia heard his sister's embarrassing announcement that he admired her? Or only his equally embarrassing lie that he found Olivia's company unpleasant? What if she believed it?

Even if she had heard nothing, it was rather obvious he and Amelia had been talking about her. Of course, she would naturally assume the worst. And explanation would only reveal far more embarrassing emotions. Sometimes his own capacity for stupidity amazed even him.

He should check the bricks one last time, perhaps, but instead he merely stood there, leaning his head on the cool, lacquered edge of the sled.

Ten

By the time the party had made their way out of the house and sorted themselves into sleds, Olivia had serious doubts as to the happy conclusion of the affair. The party of younger people had set off ahead, laughing and singing, and she, relegated to the group of gouty squires and dropsical dowagers, was forced to keep the peace in the second sled.

"I hope you've had the sense to send men down to find the Yule log," Lady Toby snapped, attempting to keep her enormous woolen toque from flying off her head in the brisk breeze, "and I hope it isn't too far away." She released her grip on the hat to wag a forefinger under Lord Harrow's nose.

Under his aunt's glare, the poor man had dutifully given up his seat in the fashionable sled for the one containing the most titles. Of course, Harrow was too well bred to show any disappointment.

She had to credit him with that. He tolerated his aunt's bullying just as he put up with her during their outings to see the improvements. She recalled the innumerable times she'd made barbed comments, been coldly condescending, been outright rude. But he'd always cheerfully put up with it. Somehow she'd thought— Well, she'd thought in some way he'd grown to enjoy their interaction. But she had heard him, plain as day, telling his sister he didn't.

Oh, why couldn't she remember the honey-and-vinegar principle? Though he sat directly across from her, their knees almost touching, Harrow seemed unaware of her gaze. She had always thought of him as open and frank, but now he was impossible to read.

"Why, I remember a time when Lord Allingsworth had a Yule log expedition, and he didn't remember where last year's log was," Lady Toby went on. "We spent hours searching about for it. By the time we decided to give up and go home, I was nearly blue with cold. Who would invite people over for a Yule log expedition without having planned it? Rude, that's what it is. Thinking we have nothing better to do than ride about in freezing weather."

Harrow was merely smiling and nodding at Lady Toby, just as jovial and laughing as he was when Olivia herself was being difficult.

Why did she care if he enjoyed their outings, she chastised herself. They were for education, not pleasure.

But she had grown to enjoy them. And stupidly, she had rather thought he looked forward to them as well. She raised her chin. Well, enough was enough. She would finish showing Harrow her father's accomplishments as quickly as possible and then insist that he reinstate Papa at the new year.

Lady Toby jabbed Olivia in the ear with her elbow as she wrestled with her capricious toque. "Don't you agree, Miss Faraday? I'm sure you don't have any interest in catching your death while we search the world for a lump of wood."

Olivia came back to the matter at hand and gave Harrow a look. Had he planned for this outing? Was it possible that he didn't know that a Yule log had to be cut the year before? One couldn't simply dash out into the woods and chop down a tree. It wouldn't be dry enough. It would never burn.

"I'm sure your aunt knows where last year's was cut," she said reassuringly. She had no idea if the Harrow family had ever had a Yule log. They'd certainly never had an outing to gather it in. She felt a momentary flash of anger. Why had the servants let him go on in ignorance? They knew he was new to this. They should have known he needed guidance.

"Well, sirrah?" Lady Toby demanded, turning back from where she had been carrying on a separate, parallel argument with Lord Toby over whether it had been appropriate to take the decanter of port from the sideboard and bring it with them.

"Our intention today should be merely to enjoy the company and the fine weather," Olivia heard herself say cheerfully. Lady Toby rolled her eyes and went back to arguing with Lord Toby. She shot Harrow a glance but he was smiling pleasantly, unconcerned. She saw, however, that one knee was bouncing up and down in an anxious dance.

"Well, if we should happen to be unable to find last year's log," she said to him quietly, "I know where another is. I've seen it lying in the woods for several years and always thought it would be perfect for a Yule log."

He gave her a look of pretend shock. "Is there an actual log involved? How perfectly rustic you country people are."

What unbearable impertinence. She snapped her head away, feeling a rush of embarrassment. Fine. Let the man be humiliated.

Ahead of them, the guests in the first sled started a

riotous Christmas carol. She could hear Susanna's ringing laugh above the others'. Now, why couldn't Harrow have sat in her sister's sled? Susanna would charm him. He would no longer smile at her, and then the uncomfortable feeling behind her ribs would ease.

"Oh dear," Reverend Eggart said in a querulous voice as he pulled his muffler up to his eyebrows, "it looks like it will snow."

"Snow!" Lady Toby exclaimed. "We must turn around at once. We shall be lost in the woods and freeze to death."

"Nonsense," Lord Toby returned. "The temperature is perfect."

"That's only because we are so crowded together," Eggart grumbled.

She saw Harrow's shoulder shaking and watched him flush with suppressed laughter.

"My dear Miss Faraday," he said, his eyes twinkling, as always. "If you insist on pressing your lips so tightly together you will do yourself injury. Here—" He leaned very close to her and for an alarming moment she thought he actually meant to kiss her or some such thing. Then she realized with a fierce blush that he was merely reaching into a pocket of his coat. He produced a flask.

"More of my aunt's excellent rum punch," he said, extracting a glass from the basket at his feet and offering to pour her a tot. "We must get you into the Christmas spirit by hook or by crook."

"No, thank you," she said primly.

"Go on, girl," Lord Toby said, pouring himself a generous portion. "Lady Toby has drunk nearly the whole decanter from the salon."

In order to avoid the inevitable row that would follow, Olivia took a small glass.

"How does your family usually celebrate Christmas, Miss Faraday?" Lord Harrow asked.

He did not appear inclined to tease her now, but was merely looking at her with an expression of polite interest.

She took a large gulp of the punch and felt it burn the length of her throat. Harrow was a good listener—she had to give him that. When he listened, he had a way of making it seem that she was the only person in the universe.

Though of course it wasn't that he wore that expression of interest solely when he was listening to her, she reminded herself sternly. She'd seen him listen to her father, Frederica, and his tenants that way as well.

She could understand why he'd been popular with the ladies of London. His manners were indeed pleasing. And there was something rather appealing about that inane grin. She found herself wishing there was more space between the two of them.

"Well," she began, "when I was a child we always made wreaths and kissing boughs to decorate the house. Susanna, Christopher, Frederica, and I would roast chestnuts and play snapdragon just like all children do, I suppose." She smiled. It had all been so long ago. "Papa would make each of us a present. They were the most peculiar things, to think back on it. He is an engineer at heart and very clever with his hands.

"I had a castle made of metal plates that could be put together with pins. A puzzle, really. One year Christopher received a dragon made of wood. It had a metal case in its belly and you could put in a bit of coal so that the smoke came out of the dragon's nose. Everyone in Littleton came to see it. It was quite grand."

She realized it had been a long time since she had thought of those days. She was warm and grinning like an idiot. Perhaps it was the punch. She held out her glass for more. "Another year the four of us received our very own loom."

"Loom?" Harrow repeated, nonplussed.

"Oh yes, there was a woman down the road who wove for a living, and we became fascinated with it. So Papa made us a loom and we learned how to spin and weave. Good skills to have, really. Though of course we only turned out the most ugly, lumpy bits of cloth."

Again he was looking at her intently. As though he actually cared a farthing about what she'd done for Christmas. "And your mother?" he asked. "Did she participate in the festivities?"

She shook her head. It was feeling curiously light. "She died when Frederica was born. Susanna remembers her best. And Christopher. But we had a marvelous cook growing up who would make the most spectacular spread of Christmas fare. In fact, I chipped a tooth on her Christmas pudding."

"Not much of a cook," he protested.

"Oh, on the contrary," she laughed. "It happened because of my greed. I suspect the rest of my family saw her Christmas pudding as an opportunity to look for the lucky sixpence she always baked into it. But I thought it so delicious I just gobbled it up as soon as I could get my hands on it." She indicated her incisor. "See?"

Harrow leaned closer, took her chin in his hands, and inspected her mouth. "Yes, I do see. I'm delighted."

She felt her face going very hot against his gloved fingertips. This was not how Olivia Faraday behaved.

She didn't giggle and prattle and let a gentleman touch her cheek while she looked into his sea-green eyes. She pulled away and sat back against the seat. "Why?" she demanded.

He folded his arms and regarded her with amusement. "You have a flaw."

She closed her lips and scowled at him. The rum must have taken more effect than she thought, for she found she couldn't maintain it. "You, sir, are impossible."

"Good God, Harrow, she isn't a horse you're going to buy," Toby exclaimed with a loud guffaw. "If you want to court her, you'll have to be more subtle than that!" He burst into loud quacks of laughter.

Olivia likely should have given Toby a sharp set-down, as he was obviously in his cups, but she found that she was laughing along. "I'm sorry to say that Lord Harrow has found me flawed, sir. And of course he's far too discriminating a judge to take less than a diamond of the first water."

"Never mind, my dear," Toby crowed, slapping her rather hard on the knee. "You've a clever father, best land man in the country. Put Capability Brown to shame in his day. A man of science. He'll do better than let you marry this jackanapes." He slapped Harrow's knee in turn. "Find you someone clever."

She darted Harrow a look of triumph and found to her surprise that he was staring with a rather absorbed expression out into the snowy woods. Perhaps he was worried about the elusive Yule log.

"There, now," she said, hoping to turn the conversation, "I've told you all our country Christmas traditions and you must think us simpletons entirely. What of you, at Harrow End?"

He thought for a moment. "We must have grown up but a few miles from each other."

"No, I'm afraid not. We moved around a great deal in my childhood, because of my father's commissions. We only came to Littleton five years ago." For some reason she rather wished they had grown up near each other. But of course, their worlds would have remained entirely separate.

"Christmas at Harrow End must have been quite grand."

He laughed. "Not in the least. I tortured my sisters as much as your brother did his, I'm certain. We went to church; we ate too much. We played games, received presents, though very ordinary ones compared to yours, and we broke them."

He smiled a smile that contained no self-mockery or teasing, only warmth. "I have very pleasant Christmas memories. Though none were, perhaps, very memorable. The year before last at Christmas my sister announced that she was in a family way," he shrugged. "That was rather jolly. For her, I suppose."

"And last year?"

His smile was a little remote. "Just the usual, I'm afraid. We were in mourning for my father, and my uncle Lord Harrow as well, so there was very little celebration."

She felt a pang of guilt. She'd forgotten that he, too, had suffered loss. And as he had reminded her on occasion, he hadn't planned on becoming the viscount.

Perhaps he hadn't had everything he'd ever wanted after all.

Perhaps Christmas at Harrow End was celebrated with the dull grandeur that permeated everything the gentry did. Christmas at the Littleton Park estate house had been a sober enough affair. Well enough for a pompous, wellborn adult, but a child?

She had a momentary picture of Lord Harrow, doubtless a mischievous, exuberant child, following the stiff Christmas rituals of the upper class. The lord and lady would duly present gifts to the poor, boxes for the servants, something expensive and useless for gentlemen employees like her father and . . . and that was all.

Christmas in the Faraday house was sacred. In some ways the chaos, mess, and joyful hysteria of it drove her to madness. But she realized she would be lost without it.

She would ensure that this Christmas was a real Faraday Christmas. They would have oranges, hang the expense. She would complete the gingerbread army she was planning to bake for Susanna's boys. They would carol and dance and Frederica would have her Christmas wish, whatever it had changed to at the moment.

She blinked her eyes, feeling strangely sentimental. Likely the punch, she reminded herself dryly.

Jack Harrow appeared to have lost interest in discussing country Christmas traditions. He was involved in directing a groom to go and retrieve Lady Toby's hat, which had escaped her head at last. He listened to the countess swear a blue streak and assured her with admirable gravity that he was certain it had suffered no ill effects. Crisis averted, he leaned out of the sled, looked around, and directed the coachman to a far clump of trees. Olivia realized he knew very well where he was going.

"Did you think I was a complete nodcock?" he asked, looking down at her with laughing eyes.

She started to object but could not. Perhaps she *had*

had too much punch. Perhaps it was the heady freedom of being out of the house for the day. Whatever the reason, she found she could only laugh.

"You dreadful man. And to think I felt sorry for you."

"I forgive you, Miss Faraday. I'm sure the notion that I could be competent at anything eluded you."

Her tart reply died in her throat. They had come into a clearing. The servants had obviously been there to prepare. A bonfire lit up the growing dusk of the early winter evening. Already it threw bright splashes of warm light on the trees around them. A spit across the flames held steaming tins of wassail, punch, and mulled wine. They filled the air with a rich blend of allspice and cloves. Two tables had been set up with linens and lanterns and were decorated with fir boughs. They were piled high with mincemeat pies, puddings, sugarplums, and oranges. In the center of the clearing, festooned with holly and ribbons, was the Yule log.

Olivia nearly laughed aloud. This was the very tree she'd meant to lead Lord Harrow to, thinking he hadn't planned. He must have found it himself in his rambles.

How strange; she hadn't really wondered what he did during the time when he was not riding out to various sites on the estate with her. Somehow she'd vaguely imagined he was living some variation of his life in London. Drinking, gambling—certainly nothing so wholesome as riding about looking for suitable Yule logs.

Lady Westhaven came dancing over from the other sled as they got out. "Marvelous Jack! It's absolutely magical. You cannot tell me you planned this yourself. Surely you had expert advice." She shot a glance in Olivia's direction.

"Oh, no," Olivia countered. "It was not I. I'd never have dreamed of anything half so fine."

Lady Westhaven was right. It *was* magical. The bonfire sent up showers of sparks into the darkening sky, and the snow in the ring of light around it sparkled like opals. With the bright ribbons and the sumptuous clothes of the arriving guests, it was lavish beyond her imagination.

"My aunt helped," Lord Harrow admitted. "And our housekeeper. She has a marvelous ingenuity when given the freedom to create." He shot his sister a mischievous look. "I'm afraid I will further incur Aunt Alva's wrath. I arranged for the children of Littleton to come as well."

"Oh, Jack," his sister crowed. "She will have an apoplexy."

"Well, it isn't as though there isn't plenty of food," he said, raising his broad shoulders in a shrug. "And since they won't be able to participate in the Yule ball, I thought—"

Olivia was rather glad that Lady Westhaven threw her arms around her brother. If she hadn't, Olivia might have felt inclined to do so herself.

"How famous!" Lady Westhaven exclaimed. "Are the sleds going back for them? There is nothing children like so much as a sledding expedition. May I go back and escort them? I can't wait to see their faces when they see what you have done here. It's a fairyland!"

"Don't trouble yourself, Lady Westhaven, I will go," Olivia spoke up.

"No," said Harrow. "Let Amelia go. I need you here."

"Oh, yes," Lady Westhaven said, quickly. "You must stay here. Help Jack make sure everyone is comfortable."

She flitted off and left them standing alone. For a moment Olivia felt unexpectedly awkward.

"Will Miss Frederica be pleased?" Harrow asked her. "She seemed so keen to be included in the Christmas festivities. She said it was her Christmas wish."

Olivia laughed. Frederica's Christmas wish changed ever more rapidly as the day itself approached. "She will be delighted. You're very good to indulge her. To indulge all of us," she added. She didn't mean to sound so serious, and she certainly didn't mean to say it while looking into his eyes.

He said nothing, but merely smiled. It was not the inane smile, but a different, private one.

She broke the spell and turned away. She was here to make sure the guests were comfortable. Yes. She had a job to do. Lord Toby took her arm as he descended heavily from the sled. "Dashed long way to come for a drink and a pile of ladies' scrap food," he grumbled, bearing toward the tables. Christmas punch is a fine thing, but it seems a waste to wrap all this folderol about it. Ah, here's a joint. Cut me a bit of that, man."

Olivia saw to it that the man was being served, and then busied herself by helping to light candles and dish out wassail to the guests.

She approached Susanna, two cups in hand. Her sister was standing with Lord Randolf, looking intently up into a tree.

"La, no, sir," Susanna was saying. "I believe you are wrong."

Randolf was a solemn man. He was known by the neighbors to be scholarly, and grave to the point of dour. Not the kind of man who went to London for the Season, enjoyed a good country dance, or appreciated a neat ankle. Not the man for Susanna. But he was rich, he was handsome, and he was titled. And her sister was obviously doing her best.

To Olivia's surprise, the man gave Susanna a slight smile. "Indeed, I am sure of it," he said. "Botany is a specialty of mine. And," he shrugged, "rules are rules, you know."

"But surely, it doesn't count unless the mistletoe is fashioned into a proper kissing bough."

Olivia knew by the invitation in her sister's voice that disaster was eminent. Had the woman no sense?

"Spiced punch?" she offered in a ringing voice.

The couple turned to her in surprise. A look of annoyance crossed Susanna's face.

"Excellent," Lord Randolf said. His expression showed that he had no idea that Susanna had set her marital sights on him, nor that she was deadly accurate at close range. "Miss Faraday, you can help us settle a question. Do you believe that mistletoe *in situ* counts for kissing?"

"I'm certain I don't know," she said coolly.

"Really, Olivia," Susanna scolded, "what are you doing, going around with drinks like a servant? Lord Harrow has plenty of people to be certain his guests have everything they need." As she spoke a liveried footman came by with a silver tray of food.

"Yes, well, I—"

"Can't you stop, even for a moment?" Susanna hissed as soon as Lord Randolf was distracted by the business of selecting the most tempting morsels for a plate he was filling for her. "Must you always be *doing* things? Working? Meddling?"

She stared at her sister, wounded. "Someone has to work." She heard the defensiveness in her voice and cringed. She and Susanna were squabbling like they had when they were children.

"No," her sister countered, "no one has to. Not right now. You'll make Harrow feel like a bad host if you keep up your eternal fussing."

Olivia was silenced. She dutifully sipped at one of the cups and looked around. It was true. All of the other guests seemed to be perfectly content to have the servants tend to their needs while they laughed and chatted.

She inhaled the scent of nutmeg, cloves, and brandy from her steaming cup and pretended to feel as comfortable as the others appeared.

She found herself looking for Harrow. He was in cozy conversation with Lord and Lady Westhaven. As she watched, he turned to look and include Miss Eggart in the conversation. After a moment, he disentangled himself and moved on, the gracious host, to the next group of people.

She was suddenly aware that she was standing with Lord Randolf and her sister, still interrupting their flirtation.

She wandered off, wishing she knew better what to do with herself. Had she been so long out of society that she was hopelessly inept? She, who was used to being efficient and responsible, was suddenly the useless one.

Ugh. It was her Season all over again.

"Here, here," Lord Toby waddled over to her. "A load of children has just arrived. And the wretched little monkeys are about to start some infernal caroling. Nothing I can abide less than rosy, wholesome-looking little devils lisping and warbling like cats in a bag. Come with me. We'll go off hunting for holly or mistletoe or some such thing and let them caterwaul about good will toward men." He took her arm with old-fashioned ceremony and led her toward the edge of the clearing.

"Dashed silly holiday," he grumbled, eyeing a sprig of holly and considering whether it was worth soiling his gloves to obtain. "Gives young people, or even not-so-young ones, tremendous notions."

Olivia glanced over her shoulder to where her sister had evidently given up on Lord Randolf and returned to her admirer Lord Pennyworth. The two were now loudly pursuing other guests with their makeshift kissing bough. It was eliciting a great many squeals of false protest among the younger guests.

"Indeed," she said, trying to recall if she'd ever been caught beneath the kissing bough with anyone who wasn't the most benign of male relatives. She pushed away all ridiculous wishes.

"Always been that way," he continued, at last gingerly snapping off the sprig of holly and presenting it to her with elaborate gallantry. "Too much drinking and singing and romance. Proposed to Lady Toby at a Twelfth Night ball," he continued. "Deadly combination of rum punch and holiday sentimentality. Never known a moment's peace since."

He shot his wife a curmudgeonly look of affection. Lady Toby launched into a carol with the others. Lord Toby sighed and made a dramatic show of producing the port decanter from somewhere about his capacious person. Somehow Olivia's own cup was replenished with its contents as well.

"Now you," Lord Toby waggled a finger at her. "You're a clever girl—less of a nuisance than most young ladies. Had the sense to brush off that old maid in trousers, Reverend Eggart. You look after your father like a good girl and there's never a peep of trouble out of you."

Olivia began to laugh. The man was quizzing her. "Oh, I'm certain I shall be a great deal of trouble. I merely thought I would wait until Easter."

"I'll drink to that," he said, upending his glass. "Less Christmas nonsense—particularly those carols—and more Christmas spirits."

Olivia looked up. The stars were bright now, and so close that they seemed hung like tin ornaments in the tree branches above them. In the clearing she could hear Frederica explaining in great detail to Lady Westhaven her most remarkable luck with Christmas wishes. Someone called for more mince pies.

She felt a bit giddy. She could very nearly forget about Papa, the estate, the accounts, and Lord Harrow's maddening presence in their lives. At the moment, they all seemed like snowflakes that would melt away. She linked her arm with Lord Toby's and touched her cup to his. "Indeed," she echoed with gusto. "To less Christmas nonsense."

Eleven

Jack looked around to be sure the Yule log expedition was progressing to his aunt's satisfaction. There didn't appear to be any imminent disasters. The servants were graciously allowing the guests to hinder them with enthusiastic participation as they rolled the great Yule log onto a sledge in preparation for dragging it back to the house. The wassail was flowing and everyone, despite his earlier misgivings, appeared to be enjoying themselves.

There, let Olivia see that he had at least a modicum of breeding. Though she was hardly likely to be impressed with his ability to throw a party, he reminded himself. Where was she? Likely she'd discovered he'd done something all wrong and had gone off in her eternal efficient, practical way to fix it.

He saw his aunt towing over yet another sweet young blossom. Good Lord. The woman was as much of a matchmaker as his own mother. Devil take it, he was half tempted these days to pick the most ineligible woman he could find, marry her, and be done with it. He tried to imagine the looks on their faces when he introduced some dairymaid as the next Lady Harrow. Or some industrialist's daughter. Or some agriculturalist's. He nearly laughed aloud. Now that was comical.

He caught a glimpse of Olivia's blue cloak through

the trees. What was she doing, walking out in the woods with that old soak Lord Toby? Ignoring the rapid approach of his aunt's simpering miss, he strode in the direction of the cloak.

To his surprise, he found Miss Faraday leaning against a tree, laughing helplessly at Lord Toby as he capered about in imitation of revelers at a country dance.

"Ho ho!" Lord Toby shouted. "What's this? A kissing bough? What abominable luck!" He embraced an imaginary partner with enthusiasm.

Olivia, wiping her streaming eyes, looked up to see him staring at her. To his surprise, instead of pokering up at being caught in this undignified display of mirth, she ran to him and caught up his hands.

"I have found Lord Toby out," she exclaimed, still laughing. "He can claim all he wants that he regrets being shackled to Lady Toby, but he's wildly in love with her, and I know it."

Jack looked down at her, shocked. He knew from experience that it took a great deal of raillery to make Olivia laugh so openly. Now her cheeks were flushed, her eyes bright, and she looked like a different, indeed quite beautiful, woman.

"Indeed," he said at last, still bewildered. And then, more stupid still, "I trust you're enjoying yourself? Did you wish to join the caroling?"

For some ridiculous reason this set them off again. Lord Toby collapsed in the snow with laughter.

"Carols!" he shouted. "I shall set myself aflame like a Christmas pudding before I sing a carol."

Jack refrained from commenting acidly that the man had imbibed enough alcohol to ensure his combustibility. Instead, he watched in bemusement as the man abruptly picked himself up, dusted off the snow, and waddled off, shouting out the words to "The Holly and the Ivy."

It suddenly seemed very quiet in the fringe of woods beyond the clearing.

"It's snowing," Olivia announced, just when the silence became awkward. She craned her neck upward, exposing a long, white expanse of throat. "Just a moment ago I could see the stars and now they're covered with clouds."

He looked up to see tiny flakes spinning down from the dark sky. Nearby he could hear his guests starting another uncoordinated round of songs. He would go to them in a moment.

"What were you doing out here alone with that man?" he demanded, chiding her as he would have Amelia.

Olivia laughed her infectious laugh again. "You are very chivalrous, Lord Harrow, to be concerned for my welfare, but I assure you, my reputation was in no danger."

He frowned. The girl had likely had too much rum punch. "Miss Faraday, I must remind you that a young lady—"

"I'm not a young lady," she assured him. To belie her words she turned her face to the sky and whirled about, enjoying the snowflakes dancing down. "I must say," she went on before he could argue, "that I'm most agreeably surprised."

"With what?" he asked, bemused.

"With you." She looked down at the sprig of holly she was holding in her hand and then came over and tucked it in his buttonhole. Again he was stunned by her smile. "I had forgotten what it was like to have such a lovely time."

"You are too serious," he said, glad to find her in such

a receptive mood. He wondered if there was a polite way to tell her that she looked far prettier when she was laughing than when she wore her usual somber expression.

"And you," she said, poking a slender forefinger into his cravat, "are not serious enough."

Tipsy, he assured himself. She never would have allowed herself to admit to enjoying herself otherwise. Tomorrow she would pay for it. And, of course, he reminded himself, so would he. She would likely redouble her shrewishness in an effort to prove that this pleasant, flirtatious . . . attraction was merely a fermentation byproduct.

"A serious man," she continued, jabbing at him again, "would not allow his guests to get so boisterous." She indicated with a gesture toward where Lord Toby was now attempting to ride atop the Yule log. "Ow!"

Jack looked down to see that she'd pricked her finger on the holly in his buttonhole. She stared for a moment at the spot of crimson welling up on her fingertip. Then, like a child, she put her finger in her mouth.

"Don't do that," he said quickly, embarrassingly aware that his body had immediately tightened with desire at the innocent act. He pulled her hand away. Her gesture was not one a gently bred young lady should make, particularly if she was standing, nearly secluded in a grove of trees, looking deliciously vulnerable as the snow settled lightly on the intricate twists of her uncovered hair.

"A serious man," she continued, watching with disinterest as he twisted his handkerchief around the minuscule wound on her finger, "would not invite guests of such awkward, disparate backgrounds."

She frowned, but did not seem overly concerned that he had retained her hand. It was cold as marble, her nails faintly bluish, so he began chafing it lightly. "Where are your gloves?" he asked. "You—"

"A serious man," she interrupted, "would not overset his aunt by unexpectedly inviting hordes of children to her party." She gave him a severe look. "A serious man would not let Susanna run amok with a kissing bough."

"I'm afraid I have no control over—"

She tilted her chin down, her bright eyes steady on his own. Her free hand came up to prod at his cravat again, so he captured that one, too. Her brows came together, but her eyes remained locked with his. "A serious man would not let his lady guests kiss him."

He jerked back, wounded. "I protest. Miss Faraday, I have not—"

Her pretty lips curved into an utterly innocent, utterly captivating smile. "But you are not serious," she whispered.

And then she rose quickly on her toes and pressed her mouth briefly to his.

She'd kissed him. Gentle and light as a snowflake. The hair stood up on the back of his neck. For all his conniving, his wishing, his fantasizing as to how to accomplish it without deriving immediate bodily harm afterwards, she'd been the one to do it.

He half expected her to come to her senses now and wallop him for letting her do something she would so obviously regret. Instead she still stood there, toe-to-toe with him in the snow, her face rosily triumphant. "My first kiss," she said.

No, no, no.

He might have even said the words aloud. His throat was tight, his skin on fire. With one movement, he pulled the slender hands he retained, and when she swayed closer, he wrapped his arm around her waist. He paused for a moment. Her pulse was leaping at the base of her neck, as quickly as his own. Her face, as though she didn't realize this was actually happening, was unafraid.

He kissed her, this time a real kiss. A kiss that involved pressure and passion, exploration. One that left her no choice but to respond in kind. She tasted faintly of buttered rum and sugarplums. He hadn't intended to kiss her so long, or with any sort of intimacy. He hadn't expected her to kiss him back.

Finally, when he found that his hands had started to take entirely inappropriate license, he pulled away. "There," he panted. He took her by the shoulders. "Now, I told you I was going to do it. Or I didn't exactly tell you, but you knew I would. So you can't fly at me." His heart was pounding hard in his ears as he waited for her to box them.

Instead she merely stood there, looking slightly stunned.

Over his shoulder he could hear his guests calling for him. He gripped Olivia more tightly by the shoulders. "Stay here and count to one hundred. Do you hear me? Then come into the clearing. I don't believe you want everyone to know."

To his relief, he saw a snap of irritation spring back into her unfocussed eyes. "You needn't act as though I'm an idiot. Of course I understand you."

He grinned down at her with what he knew must be unbearable impertinence and then turned to walk away with the pleasure of that kiss still singing through him.

Twelve

Olivia pressed her lips together and watched as her sister made an inarticulate noise of frustration and then threw up her hands with a gesture of disgust.

"Papa," Susanna said, "I told you he was coming to call, and I told you to be on your best behavior." She stood up and stalked across to the window where the stiff back of Lord Randolf could be seen riding away.

With another gesture of aggravation she whirled back on her father. "You knew very well that he was Lord Cedric Randolf's son, and yet you deliberately pretended you didn't know him. I'm certain he thinks you mad. What were you talking about? All that nonsense about money stashed away. It's all been spent. There isn't any money. Our man of business wrote me to say that any savings is long gone. Gone! Am I right, Olivia?"

"There is no money," Olivia said dully.

Susanna gestured toward her with a kind of hysterical triumph. "See? No money. And then to accuse Randolf of stealing your shoes! Oh Papa, I've never been so humiliated in my entire life."

Olivia felt genuine sympathy for her sister. Or at least all the sympathy she could muster through a crippling headache. What had she been thinking, drinking all that Christmas punch?

Papa was having one of his bad days, and Lord Randolf had obviously not been briefed ahead of time. Susanna and Olivia had had their hands full trying to carry on a semblance of a normal visit while Papa kept interrupting with demands that they explain the man's presence in their house. Then he'd gone off in a rambling discourse about planting, drainage systems, Christopher, and the missing shoes.

Susanna dashed away tears of anger. "It was awful, Papa. Just awful. I should have told him that you were too ill to see him, but Olivia said you would be interested in meeting my new beau." She turned on them both, her beautiful face screwed into an expression of hatred. "An earl! I could have been a countess, but for you."

"I thought you liked Pennyworth," Olivia said unwisely.

Susanna gave her a look of distain. "A younger son? Really, Olivia, I must be practical. But Randolf would have proposed. An earl! And now I shall never get married!"

"There are other earls in the world," she suggested.

Her sister pressed her hands to her face. "But I wanted that one!" She turned in a whirl of petticoats and slammed the door on her way out of the study.

Olivia drew a steadying breath. Of course Susanna was overreacting, but she couldn't really blame her. How would she have felt if Papa had acted that way with someone she cared about?

She ignored the sudden ache under her ribs and went to her father. He looked up at her, his sunken cheeks pale. "What's happening?" he demanded in the thin, confused voice that he'd been using too often these days.

What *was* happening? Papa had been doing so well. She'd been sure he was recovering. Hadn't he been? He'd been talking more about the estate lately. And he seemed interested in hearing what Harrow thought of his improvements. If only Harrow would keep him on, he would surely improve. His work had always been his passion. Harrow *must* keep him on.

"Is Mama going to leave us here?" a voice asked from beneath the side table.

Olivia jumped. "George! Teddy! Come out from under there. Were you back there the whole time? I thought Frederica was minding you." Good Lord, any more of this and she would run screaming out of the house.

Her two nephews tumbled out onto the carpet. "Mama said that if she didn't have a beau by the new year, she'd go off to London again," Teddy volunteered.

His brother wiped his runny nose on his sleeve and looked as though he might burst into tears again. "She said she wouldn't take us with her. She said she hadn't the money for us all to go."

"And now Mama's gentleman left, and so now she's going to leave us."

Olivia left her father's side to go and comfort the boys. "Your mama isn't going to leave you," she said, hoping it wasn't a lie. "We'll all stay right here."

"I don't like it here," Teddy objected. "The mutton Molly makes is all stringy, and I miss my pony."

"Oh, dearest—"

"And Grandpapa smells funny," George added in a stage whisper.

Olivia forced back a laugh and hugged them to her. "Now, boys. You know you shouldn't be in here spying on your Mama's visitors. What would she say if she knew? She'd be very disappointed that you weren't on your best behavior. I know she has some lovely Christmas presents planned for you. You don't want to make her so cross that she forgets to give them to you, do you?"

It was weak to resort to threats, but her head was aching so badly she truly couldn't think of anything else. How stupid she'd been to drink so much punch! She was a grown woman, not some green girl getting tipsy on a glass of ratafia over dessert.

And that kiss. A pain lanced through her when she thought of it. Foolishness upon foolishness. And with Lord Harrow, of all people! The very man she should have avoided.

"Olivia, what are those boys doing here?" her father demanded querulously. "Boys should be outdoors, playing with the dogs and horses in the stables, running races, making mischief."

"Papa," she reminded him in a low voice, "it's snowing outside." She refrained from commenting that the stable had been empty of dogs and horses except poor Gerald and Trueheart for the last year, and that the boys had indeed been making mischief.

"Nonsense," he said, his tone as imperious as it had been in the old days. "Get them out of here. Underfoot! Can't abide it. If Christopher finds them here he'll thrash 'em."

"No, Aunt 'Livia!" Teddy set up a wail and his brother followed suit. "Don't make us go. I'm tired of the nursery. It's too cold and Frederica says she's bored reading our storybooks to us."

"Olivia, take them out of here. I don't like the noise. If they're beggars, give them a few pennies and send them off. They can beg at the next house. Or better yet, at Littleton Park. Lord Harrow will find some employ-ment for them. Now where is Christopher?"

"Don't send us off! Don't send us off!" the boys were leaping about like grease in a pan, apparently convinced that they were truly in danger of being mistaken for beg-gar children and sent off into the snow.

Olivia, still squatting down with the boys, pressed her hands to her temples and reminded herself that it would do little good to scream.

"Miss Faraday," Molly said quietly from the doorway. "You have a visitor."

"Not now, Molly. I'm having a crisis."

From her crouched position on the floor she saw Lord Harrow's highly polished Hessians cross the carpet to her. Lovely. This was all she needed.

"Hello," she said and looked up and smiled brightly at Lord Harrow's handsome face. "You're really not wanted here right now."

"I know," he said with abominable cheer. "But I'm here nonetheless."

She made a noise that sounded embarrassingly like a growl and stood to her feet. "I can't take you riding on the estate today. I've too much else to take care of."

Please let him have forgotten yesterday. No—better yet, please let it have been merely a false memory, a fantasy brought on by all that wretched wassail.

"This is merely a social call," he said, drawing him-self up a little awkwardly.

"We are not at home," she fired back, the memory, all too real, blazing painful streaks through her. Like a brazen hussy, she'd let him kiss her. No—worse, she'd kissed him. She'd thrown herself at him. The headache that had been drumrolling all day burst into a tympani crescendo.

"Ah," Susanna breezed into the room, wearing a fresh new gown, all traces of her former fury replaced by a delighted smile. "Lord Harrow! How fortunate that you have found us at home."

She should have been glad that her sister had appeared. Susanna would ensure that Harrow's attention was drawn away from her. She would leave Olivia free to soothe the still-hysterical boys and pacify her father, who continued to demand her attention in a querulous tone.

Instead she felt something that was shamefully like jealousy.

Harrow bowed over Susanna's hand and then crossed to greet her father. He seemed pleasant, ordinary. Just as though yesterday had never happened. "I must thank you, sir, for letting us enjoy the company of your three daughters yesterday," he said.

"I have three daughters. Susanna, Olivia, and Frederica," her father confirmed. Oh heavens, but Papa was really not in good form today.

"Lord Harrow, you must allow us to thank you for inviting us," Susanna chirruped. "We had such a marvelous time. I can't think of when I enjoyed an outing more. Why, it's enough to make one like the country." Her sister moved over to sit in the chair beside Papa, in order to better look up into his lordship's green eyes, Olivia suspected.

"Though I must protest that you were wrong not to warn me about Lord Randolf." Susanna's chin went up. "He's not nearly as gentlemanly as I thought. You should have protected me."

"Oh," Harrow said, looking uncomfortable. "Thought things were going well there." He shot Olivia a glance. She quickly pretended to be engaged in providing handkerchief assistance to the two boys.

"Perhaps you and I might help to alleviate Miss Fara-day's crisis, Mrs. Clarke," he said. "Your sons appear to require your attention, and I could help your sister with your father's needs."

Susanna's brows drew together in a look of confusion. "I'm sure they're fine. Olivia is— Oh, very well. I'll go to them. Do Georgie and Teddy want their mummy?"

"I want Aunt 'Livia to read us a story," George asserted.

"Oh, very well, then." She turned, beaming, back to Harrow. "See, they want Olivia. Would you like to go for a walk?"

He sighed and looked rapturously at Susanna. "What a pretty picture it must be when you read to them," he said. "I can imagine all three of you together, the picture of domestic bliss."

The nausea Olivia had been fighting all morning came back in a bilious rush.

Olivia was leading the boys out of the room when Susanna detached their hands from hers and inserted herself between them. "We'll be in the drawing room," she said, visibly preening. "And you can see the pretty picture for yourself when you have settled Papa."

When the door closed it was suddenly quite quiet. Papa seemed to have lost track of their presence and had lapsed into his customary thoughtful silence.

Olivia knew she should thank Lord Harrow for inviting her to the Yule log outing. But at the same time she didn't want to remind him of what had happened. What a time for a lapse in judgment!

"How are you feeling today, sir?" Jack asked, turning his attention to her father. "It's good to see you again. I'm Beauford Harrow's nephew," he prompted, when the man's blank look continued.

"Yes, yes," her father said irritably. "Heard you were a wastrel."

"I am indeed." Jack grinned. "But your daughter has been most helpful in curing that."

Olivia kept her head down and busied herself in building up the fire. Harrow saw what she was doing and shot her a look of agony. Odious man. For one day couldn't he leave her alone in her headache and humiliation? Had she actually kissed him?

"Doubt even *she* could do that," her father muttered.

"I've been looking around Littleton Park," Harrow said, much as he did every morning. "I've enjoyed seeing your work."

Olivia did not want to hear this. She didn't want to remember that he'd gone through this polite routine every morning with no guarantee that her father would remember him. At first, she'd objected, insisting that it was insulting to talk to her father as though he was enfeebled. And sometimes her father himself objected, snapping that he knew very well who Jack was.

But of course there were other days like today where their exchange was as predictable, and her father as bemused, as when they first met.

"Did you see the French drains?" her father asked, looking boyishly eager. "Did you see the stone wall along the lane? We raised that lane, you know. Used to be sunken a good four feet. Mired half the year. We redid it in '01.

Harrow nodded with interest, just as though he hadn't had this conversation a half-dozen times.

Olivia didn't want to feel grateful to him for his kindness.

"Miss Faraday has shown me those," Harrow said.

"And the pump at the house?"

"Yes."

"And the new chickenyard?"

"Yes."

"And the orchard?"

"No," he smiled. "I haven't seen that yet."

"You've seen nearly everything," Olivia said, her voice hoarse despite her efforts to sound normal. "We shall be finished soon."

Finished. And no matter what he decided, he would be going back to London again.

He smiled as though the notion pleased him. "Well, as you've said, perhaps now is not the day to ride out to see the orchard. You look as though you aren't feeling quite the thing. Perhaps a walk?"

"No, thank you." What must he think of her? How desperate she must seem. If only he had initiated it. Then she could have been indignant. But no. He had only been a participant. Perhaps, as with her father, he was only being a polite gentleman.

She recalled how closely he had held her, bending her body backward so that it fit more tightly to his, his mouth against her, demanding. No, it hadn't been merely politeness.

"I must stay with my father," she said. Though I thank you for your kindness. Perhaps Susanna—"

"Susanna needs to spend more time with those brats of hers," her father put in unexpectedly. "Go and get your cloak, Olivia. You look white as paper. You can walk down to the orchards from here. Show him the drying house. Harrow, push me closer to the fire—it's too cold in here."

Olivia went to collect her cloak from its peg in the kitchen. She noted with annoyance that her hands were shaking. How ridiculous. She and Harrow were both sensible adults, not romantic children. They both knew there was a great deal of difference between a kiss and some silly notion of love. She shook herself. Yes, a great deal of difference.

Thirteen

When Jack reached the hallway, Teddy and George came tumbling from the drawing room and attached themselves to his leg.

"Where are you going, sir?" one of them demanded. He suspected it was Teddy, as he had recently most conveniently acquired an identifying scrape on his forehead.

"Where is your mother?" he countered.

"She waited and waited for you, but she's gone upstairs with the headache. She says we always bring on the headache. I don't like this house. Everyone is always telling us to behave. I want to go home."

Poor devils. They had no other home to go to.

"Come for a walk with your aunt and me," he said impulsively. "It will shake the kinks out of you. Go and find your coats."

"Lord Harrow," Mrs. Clarke exclaimed from the top of the stairs. "Were you looking for me?"

She looked strikingly beautiful in a day dress of deep gray. But there was a predatory look on her drawn face. It appeared that things had fallen apart with Randolf, and she was moving down *Burke's Peerage,* looking for a second choice.

"Miss Faraday and I were going to go look at the

drying house in the orchard. Would you mind if your sons accompanied us?"

Susanna Clarke looked unsure if she should be insulted that she was being excluded from an outing that she obviously found unappealing. She recovered quickly, however, and gave him a dazzling smile. "Of course," she said. "The boys adore you, you know. In fact, just the other day Georgie was saying that if he was to have another papa, it would be you."

Jack concealed his horror. "They must miss their father," he said, choosing not to address her comment directly.

"I didn't say that," George piped up.

"Lord Harrow's horses are not nearly as fine as Papa's," his brother added, as though that set the nail in the coffin.

"Do you know, Lord Harrow," Mrs. Clarke said, ignoring the children, "I am rather sorry that I insisted Frederica accompany us to Bedford the other day."

"Why is that?" He'd rather enjoyed having the scamp along. He'd helped her pick out the Norwich shawl she intended to give Olivia for Christmas. They'd decided on one that was pretty, but sensible. Rather like Olivia herself.

Mrs. Clarke lowered her lashes over her splendid blue eyes. "If we had been alone, perhaps there would have been a scandal," she said in a low voice.

He was beginning to get that hunted feeling, like when he was at a ball and a chit started flapping her fan about, making arch comments and laughing with her teeth showing.

"And then you might feel compelled to offer for me," Susanna continued, coming down a step, descending in for the kill. "Would you have found that so very terrible, Lord Harrow?"

He stuck a finger between his neck and his cravat, and attempted to make some breathing space. "You wouldn't like being married to me, Mrs. Clarke. I've been told with great authority that I am a rattle and a wastrel. You deserve better than that, I'm sure."

She came a step closer, and he found himself retreating. "There will be many more eligible, more elegant, and more titled men at the skating party tomorrow night," he reminded her. "And still more at my aunt's Yule ball. I think it is far too early for you to regret not being forced into marriage with me."

He saw the look of consideration in her eyes and gave a shaky laugh. "You'll thank me later," he added quickly. "I'm sure of that. Now, my boys! Where are your coats? It's as cold as the dowager Marchioness of Blenheim out there. You'll need all the clothes you've got." Chattering madly, he made his way toward the kitchen gardens where he and Olivia generally started their rambles.

That was a close run thing. If he wasn't very careful he'd find himself leg-shackled. He recalled that this was why he spent his time in London in the gaming hells and boxing salons. He wasn't cut out to do the pretty. And he certainly wasn't cut out for married life.

In a way he was glad not to have to face Olivia alone. If there was anyone else who appeared unwilling to do the pretty today, it was she. If her pale, pinched face was any indication, she was suffering from a nasty case of post-wassail megrims.

The little gorgon was undoubtedly regretting her momentary lapse of judgment in the woods. And if he knew anything about her it was that any show of weakness in the form of kindness was followed by a proportional backlash in ill temper. She'd cultivated her prickly exterior so no one would know what a sweet creature she was at the core. But any hint that he knew of her vulnerability, and she would string him up like a Christmas garland.

He smiled as he tromped out toward the garden with the boys. Devil fly away with the consequences. It had been worth it.

Olivia greeted the boys with pleasure and perhaps a measure of relief as well. She likely didn't wish to see him alone either. They set off toward the orchard, the boys in tow.

It was rather charming to see her with the children. She was an entirely different person. He watched her as she listened with interest to their lengthy explanation of the various bumps and bruises they had recently inflicted on each other, and praised them to the skies for the ill-formed snow angels they made beside the path. She conceded graciously to Teddy's demand that he be piggybacked, not even complaining when the boy expressed his delighted terror by grabbing pale brown fistfuls of her careful new hairstyle.

George clamored that he be carried as well, so Jack obediently allowed the boy to climb onto his own back and they set off toward the orchard.

"Your father seemed well today," he offered, tentatively trying out the territory.

Olivia scowled. "Indeed," she said tersely. "Hold me a little less tightly about the neck, Teddy, if you please. A great horseman must have light hands."

"I want a pony. A real pony," he qualified.

"Perhaps someday," she said. "Not this year. Perhaps a cockhorse in the meantime?"

"For Christmas?" George shouted. "We always get presents for Christmas."

Jack could not resist grinning at her as the boys launched into a recitation of the copious gifts they required for happiness.

"What do you want, sir?" George leaned over and peered into his face.

"For Christmas?" he asked. "I want my aunt's Yule ball not to be a disaster." He laughed. "And I want your Aunt Olivia to attend."

"Aunt 'Livia?" they exclaimed in unison, slightly appalled that he would consider inviting a female, even one so tolerable as Aunt Olivia. "What about me?"

"No," he said cheerfully.

"What about me?" Teddy called out.

"Absolutely not." He broke into a jouncing trot, much to the boy's squealing delight. "You would eat all the ices."

"Ices?" they shouted. "Bring us back ices! Go to the party and bring us back ices, Auntie."

Perhaps it was merely that George was strangling him, but he felt as though he could not quite draw breath. It was strangely important to him that she say yes.

"Yes, yes," she said with a laugh. "Of course I will bring you ices."

They were in the orchard now, and George was wiggling to be set down. He allowed the boy to slide down and join his brother in scampering like monkeys up the first suitable tree.

Bereft of something to do with his hands, he felt suddenly awkward. He wished they'd gone riding instead. At least then he would have felt competent. And she wouldn't be standing so dashed close. The memory of her in his arms illuminated his mind like a magic lantern show. He forced his attention away. If she chose to pretend nothing had happened, he would, too.

"This is the orchard." She gestured toward the rows of trees around them as though she had doubts as to his ability to identify where they were. "The trees were planted before my father's time. And before your uncle's. But my father converted the mill into a drying house. It is one of the things of which he's most proud."

The trees, planted in tidy rows, were silvered with frost. The black branches stood out as the only contrast in the misty grayness of the world around them. While yesterday's snow had stopped, there was still a lingering fog in the air. It felt as though they were the only people existing in this silent, white world.

Olivia indicated that he and the boys should follow her. A large stone mill house built by the banks of the river slowly coalesced out of the mist. The river had frozen over weeks ago, and the old water wheel stood trapped in the ice, as though it was caught unawares in the middle of its work.

The mill house was a plain stone structure, obviously at least a century old, but tidy and well-kept. Olivia led them into a low, square room. It likely had once been used for grain, but now held only a large table. Empty crates were stacked neatly along the walls.

"This is the preparation room," she said, calm and efficient as always. "In the spring and summer, we bring the fruit here, cut and pit it, and put it in the drying trays."

He should care; he knew he should. But it was very hard to concentrate today. His mind kept wandering as he obediently examined the crates and trays, making the expected noises of appreciation.

How had he never noticed before what long and perfect hands she had? He had been mad ever to deem her plain. She was lovely when she laughed. But of course she wasn't laughing now. Instead she wore that intense, intelligent expression she had when she was explaining something about the estate.

"Look, look," Teddy called. "Come look at the big wheely thing."

He followed Olivia into the round room. It had housed the mill itself. A daunting tangle of cogs and wheels connected the shaft of the mill wheel outside to a peculiar contraption in the center of the room. Instead of the millstone, there was a set of vertical wheels, each spoked with wire baskets.

"The drying room," she said, gesturing. "The water wheel turns the shaft, which rotates the drying trays around. Each tray passes continually by this trench in the floor where coals are set. The heat dries the fruit and preserves it. Littleton produces nearly five hundred pounds of dried fruit each year."

What the devil would anyone want with five hundred pounds of dried fruit? He made an enthusiastic noise to indicate that he was extremely impressed.

"Your uncle always gave a portion of the fruit back to the tenants and villagers who'd been hired to harvest it. It helps a great deal for those who have little. I'm sure that your man of business will show you that the rest of your dried fruits and berries have made you a tidy profit."

"It's ingenious," he said, pushing a tray to watch it pivot.

"The rod here catches each basket and flips it around, so that the fruit is shaken and dries more evenly."

He considered the contraption for a moment. "You must be very proud of your father."

She turned on him, suddenly very serious. "You understand then, how important it is that he keep his position?"

The boys, who were engaged in pushing drying racks around, did not appear to notice that the atmosphere in the room had grown noticeably tense.

"He's not well, Olivia."

She crossed her arms defensively across her chest. She wore that freezing expression that boded ill. "You will find no one better."

"I know that. And dash it all, it frustrates me as much as you. But you know I will have to replace him. He is not able to work."

"But it is all he has," she insisted, her voice going shrill. "Without his work he is lost. You've seen how he is—"

Her frustration, her desperation—they reminded him of the letters he received every day. Always from people who wanted something, who felt it was their right to demand that he fix things.

"I will give your father a pension," he said. "I've always told you that. Though why you insist on believing—"

Her pale face grew flushed and her fingers tightened on her crossed arms. She stepped up to him. "It isn't just about the pension," she hissed. "It is about his self-respect. He loves the estate; it is everything to him. If you pension him off and give him nothing to do, he will . . . he will fade away."

"He is already fading away, Olivia."

"No," she said quickly. "No." Her breath was coming fast, ruffling the fur edge of her blue cloak. "He is better now. He is better when he has the estate to think about. You've heard him. It's all he talks about. It is what keeps him focused. I will not allow you to take the position away from him."

He ached for her, but he was angry, too. If she didn't want the money, what else was he supposed to offer? Money was enough of a headache. Now she wanted him to cure her father?

"There is nothing I can do for your father's health," he said. "There is nothing anyone can do. I will give your father an ample pension for you to retain your position in society, I assure you."

He looked down at her. Her eyes were so pale. He used to think them emotionless, but now he could see every thought in her mind. "You need him," she said urgently. "You cannot manage Littleton without him."

"It matters very little what I need. I will have to learn to get on without him. Unfair as it is, he is not capable of managing the estate. And I know you will say that I cannot do it, either. But you're wrong."

He took her by the upper arms and forced her to look at him. He knew she was disappointed in him. Couldn't she see how hard he was trying? He felt a wave of irrational anger. "I've put up with your mockery, your martyrdom, and your superior sense of duty and responsibility in order to do right by this estate. And while I know I will make mistakes, I will study it, get advice, learn until I am capable. I will not let Littleton Park fall to pieces. You know all about duty, Miss Faraday. And my duty is not to your father—it lies with the estate."

"You owe my father more than merely a pension," she shot back. "He's made this estate what it is. The improvements have given you the income to live your life as a gentleman of means and you take away his ability to live as a gentleman at all."

He dropped his hands from her arms. It was useless. She didn't understand.

"Well, what is it that you expect me to do to pay him back?" he said, the sarcasm in his voice edged with a bitter frustration. "Marry you?"

He shouldn't have said it. He knew as soon as the words were out of his mouth that he shouldn't have. Gentlemen did not joke of such things.

He was suddenly aware that the two Clarke boys had left off their play and were watching the scene with interest.

Olivia drew a long breath at last. It sounded very loud in the silence. "I would never marry a man like you."

"I apologize, Olivia. I should not have said that. I mean, I should not have said it that way." He felt his cheeks tingling with blood as his throat tightened. "I— after yesterday . . . That is— I've been thinking—" No, he hadn't been thinking. He wasn't thinking now. He was only spilling out sloppy words, unable to escape the thoughtless blunder he'd just committed. "I was thinking that marriage to me would solve some of your difficulties."

"No."

"I mean, I would marry you. Willingly. I only meant that I thought you would never consent to marry me. Even if it would help your family." Who was this blithering idiot? Dear God, he should just take a rock and dash his own brains out before he committed more insult.

"No."

"Olivia, I— If I thought you actually would have considered it, I would have asked. I mean, I *am* asking." He looked up at the ceiling, wishing a thunderbolt would mercifully strike him down. "Will you marry me, Olivia?"

She looked him over with disgust. "That was the most pathetic excuse for a proposal I've ever heard."

"Please . . ."

The color was high in her cheeks and her fingers were clenched tightly at her sides, as though she were only with great effort controlling the urge to violently draw his claret. The two boys stared at their formerly indulgent and cheerful aunt in openmouthed astonishment.

She narrowed her eyes. "You think that merely because I—I—forgot myself yesterday, that I would jump at your offer to step graciously down to raise me from the gutter. Well, no, thank you, my lord. You and your kind have never known how to work hard, and you have never known what it is to want. I hate you and everything you represent. I would rather starve in the street with my family than accept a proposal of marriage made out of pity."

He felt humiliation settle in the pit of his stomach. "I don't pity you," he said quickly. There was no way to convince her now. There likely never had been. He turned around, unable to face her. "I just thought . . . Well, perhaps I didn't think. Just as you've always suspected, I didn't think."

The chance was lost. There was nothing to do now but beat a hasty retreat. "I'm sorry," he said, knowing she would never realize how much.

She sputtered for a moment, obviously finding she had much more to say against his character, but unable to determine what to name first. At last she turned away. "Let us forget this unfortunate moment happened. Boys, do stop playing with that. You'll pinch your fingers." The boys released the wheel and scuttled over to a safe position by the doorway. She went to them and smoothed their hair. "Come, it's cold here. Let's go back to the house. We shall have Molly make up some hot chocolate to warm you." She made to herd them out.

She had not liked him when he was a frivolous, irresponsible town buck, too easy with his laugh, too careless in his ways. But when she looked back at him, he could see clearly in her basilisk glare that now she truly despised him.

Fourteen

"My dear," Mr. Faraday said gently, "must you be quite so forceful?"

Olivia looked up from where she was pounding gingerbread dough. "Sorry, Papa," she muttered. "I didn't mean to disturb you." There was a very clear indentation of her fist in the pale brown ball. She patted it smooth and began to roll it out on the kitchen table.

Her father smiled and went back to carefully pinching a horse into shape. His long, white hands were thin, nothing but bones held together with ropes of tendons and blue veins. But he had meticulously transformed a long row of shapeless lumps into a perfect battalion of gingerbread figures. "You've been working too hard," he said after a long pause. "I don't like it. You should hire a . . . a . . . ." He groped for the word. "A girl like the one we have." He waved his hand in frustration.

"A maid? Like Molly?" Olivia provided. "We can't afford it, Papa."

The man set the horse aside and began crafting the parts of a cannon. He'd decided they would bake the parts separately and then assemble the gun carriage afterwards so it would be freestanding.

Olivia had originally planned to bake the army as

flat pieces, but he had convinced her that a set of soldiers, horses, and guns that could actually stand would be far more fun for the boys. It was the kind of idea he would have had in Christmases past. Before he became ill. She smiled. Perhaps this was a sign that he was getting better.

"Nonsense," he said. "We can afford another girl."

Olivia sighed. This was not a conversation she wished to have again.

"My savings," her father said, his voice growing querulous. "We'll use that until Harrow pays us on the next quarter day. And I have other projects."

She didn't wish to remind him that there were no savings. For the first few months after she'd taken over the running of the household, she'd found strange stashes of money. A handful of notes stuffed in a vase, a roll of sovereigns in a stocking at the back of a drawer, promissory notes from people long dead hidden behind dockets of letters in the desk. But that source of unexpected funds had long ago dried up.

And there were no other projects.

"What do you think of these?" she said, taking a tray of grenadiers from the oven. "Their knapsacks look a bit like humps, but I suppose they will do." It was best to turn the conversation away from money. Papa simply refused to understand that their circumstances had changed.

"Excellent," her father smiled, and for a moment he looked like the man she remembered. Her breath caught painfully in her throat, and she turned away.

Frederica stuck her head in the doorway. "Is it safe to come in?" she shouted.

"No!" Olivia replied. "Particularly not if the boys are with you."

Frederica rolled her eyes. "When will you be done? Georgie and Teddy are driving me to inanity."

"Insanity."

"Why can't Susanna mind them? Why does it always have to be me? It's so very unfair."

"As soon as Susanna is back from the shops, she will take over," Olivia assured her. "You said you didn't wish to go to the butcher's today. You said you'd rather take a turn at minding the boys."

"Well, I wish I hadn't. They're being monsters." She crossed her arms and showed no inclination to leave. "Where is Lord Harrow today?"

Olivia slammed the oven shut on the next batch of gingerbread. "He isn't coming."

"Why not?" her sister demanded. Then her eyes narrowed slyly. "Did you quarrel?"

"No, well, yes. Well, no, of course not. It isn't any of your business." She hoped it was only the heat of the oven that was making her so uncomfortable.

Frederica sauntered over to Papa. "I think Olivia's rather sweet on Lord Harrow, don't you, Papa? And wouldn't it be romantic if they married? I think it would be grand."

Olivia dumped another lot of flour into the bowl. It came out in a great lump that exploded from the bowl in a white cloud. "Nonsense," she coughed. "I detest him. Besides, I thought *you* were intending to marry him, Freddie."

Her sister nicked a bit of sugar from the table and popped it in her mouth. "I was," she said around it. "But I changed my mind. I am going to travel the world. Like Lady Hester Stanhope."

Olivia refrained from asking sarcastically who was going to finance her adventures.

"Lady Hester is a strumpet," her father announced. "I won't countenance it."

"Oh, don't worry, Papa," Frederica said, patting his cheek affectionately. "I shan't be a strumpet—I only mean that I will explore the world. Won't that be grand?"

"Why don't you start your exploring by going to see what your nephews have gotten up to?" Olivia suggested. "They've probably managed to bloody each other's noses by now."

Frederica made a face. "Very well. I wish Lord Harrow would come. I heard his aunt was to have a skating party tonight, and I wondered if I am invited."

"Honestly, Freddie, you can go skating any time. What could possibly be amusing in going to a party with a crowd of aristocratic bores?"

Her sister tossed her head. "Just because you have had a quarrel with Lord Harrow doesn't mean that I shouldn't have a good time," she said. "And I intend to ask him if I can be invited. Now, here is Susanna. Susanna, come and mind your boys. They're being very naughty, and I am wearied to death of them."

"Give me a moment," Susanna said crossly, putting down the basket and throwing back her hood. She went to the kitchen fire and warmed her hands. Frederica rolled her eyes and reluctantly went back to see what mischief the boys had gotten into.

"Mrs. Yarborough was quite impertinent with me," Susanna said. "And I know she gave me the skinniest chicken in the shop on purpose." She jerked loose the ties of her cloak and shrugged out of it. "And then, on the way home, I had the misfortune to run into Lord Randolf. The man barely acknowledged me."

Olivia stirred another batch of the thick dough. Her arm was aching, but she rather welcomed the opportunity to work out her annoyance. "Perhaps he dislikes seeing you flirt with every man in trousers," she said with a bit more acidity than she had meant to.

Susanna's chin went up. "Nonsense. He is merely an arrogant, cold man who hasn't the least bit of sensibility."

The countryside seemed to be rife with people like that. The kind of men who would insult a lady by offering marriage out of pity.

She wiped her fingers on her apron, and set her hands on her hips. "Honestly, Susanna, you've been making a cake of yourself. Perhaps such flirtations in town are acceptable, but here they are—"

"At least I'm trying to do something," her sister hissed.

"Do something? You mean amuse yourself? I know you're bored here. I know you're unhappy. But you won't be happy if everyone starts to cut you because you're such a terrible flirt."

Papa looked up from his endless, perfect rows of soldiers. "Susanna," he said, "I've been meaning to talk to you, girl. What is happening to my shoes? Three of them have gone missing. You must take better care of the housekeeping. I suspect the maid took them."

Susanna ignored him. "Amuse myself?" she echoed in a shrill voice. Her face was growing a mottled red. "Do you think I *want* this? Do you think I want to auction myself off? You're not the only one who can make sacrifices, Olivia."

"Olivia, tell Susanna how I've looked for my shoes."

Olivia felt a wave of shame. She had assumed her sister wished to remarry for her own comfort. She hadn't realized that she was doing it for the sake of the family.

Olivia turned out the dough and began to knead it ruthlessly. Only yesterday she herself had had an offer that would have saved their family.

Susanna wouldn't have let pride get in the way of a respectable, wealthy, loveless match. Couldn't she have done the same?

"Susanna," she said in a low voice, "I never thought—"

"I know very well I'm a burden on the family," her sister snapped. "Don't you think I know the boys have got to start school? And the only way to help is to marry again. Marry quickly and marry well."

"Susanna," Olivia said. "Don't think you must remarry when your heart is not engaged. We are not in such dire circumstances as that."

Susanna gave her a look of disbelief that conveyed a great deal.

Yes. She could have told Harrow yes. She'd bullied him with selfish words about what he owed her father and he'd offered her marriage in payment. He had obviously proposed without really thinking about it. Just words that popped out of his mouth. But she could have said yes. He would not have cried off. And how different things would have been today.

She turned back to the baking. "I'm sorry," she said. "I shouldn't have said what I did. And I'm sorry we made such a hash of things yesterday when Lord Randolf came to call."

"Randolf," Susanna said scornfully, her face going very red. "I can do better than the likes of him."

Olivia took the rolling pin and began methodically pressing the dough into a smooth sheet. "No one needs to marry anyone. We are all here together. We should stay that way. There is no need for anyone to do anything rash. Right, Papa? None of your daughters need marry for money."

Her father looked up from his work. "Indeed, Olivia,"

he said with his calm smile. "After all, we have my savings."

The sisters exchanged glances. "Yes," said Susanna with the thin smile of one who had been disillusioned many times. "And we have each other."

Fifteen

If there was anything that made Jack Harrow's flesh crawl with revulsion, it was a skating party. Skating parties were cold, dull, and utterly, predictably wholesome. It was a ball on ice without the card room to relieve the tedium. It was all the discomforts of a winter day without even the redemption of competition, excitement, or the pleasurable risk of getting oneself killed.

But Aunt Alva had decreed that there would be a skating party. So here he was, shivering in the waning light of a freezing December evening, helping the beaming Miss Eggart tie on her skates.

"Oh," that young lady said, her face suddenly collapsing into a pout, "I see you've invited the Faraday sisters. How charming. Mrs. Clarke is such a dear thing. So vivacious." She looked as though a clan of amateur bagpipers had turned up to play at her come-out ball.

Jack turned to look and was surprised to see that all three of the Faraday sisters were coming down the path, their skates over their shoulders. He'd cajoled his aunt into inviting them, of course, but had expected that Olivia would refuse this offer with as much aloof scorn as she had refused everything else he'd ever offered her.

Fool to the end, he'd even gone to the trouble of sending down a servant with express orders to sit with Mr.

Faraday for the evening. He half expected poor Mrs. Smythies to come trudging back up the hill, like the last time, smarting from the shrill dismissal she'd had from Olivia.

After all, Olivia likely believed that no one in the world could possibly take her place, even for an evening, when it came to sacrificing herself on the altar of family responsibility.

"And her sisters are so sweet as well," Miss Eggart continued, squeezing out a smile. "I thought at one point that Miss Faraday might be my sister-in-law. But my brother decided that she was perhaps not quite the kind of young lady who would be suitable for a clergyman."

She tossed her head when he did not comment. "La, you'd think Miss Frederica far too young to attend these things, but apparently it's quite acceptable. I know how you love children, Lord Harrow."

"Can't abide them, generally," he admitted. "They quite terrify me."

"But surely, someday . . ." she lowered her lashes modestly.

"Yes, yes, as you say, someday they grow up and learn to drink and play cards. I would do well to remind myself of that, Miss Eggart." He smiled placidly up at her shocked expression. He finished tying her skates and stood up to greet his new guests.

Olivia Faraday looked calm and collected, as though she hadn't just yesterday cordially invited him to take himself off to that very warm region where skating parties were never held.

He was annoyed to find that his blood was racing faster. Had he learned nothing? She'd likely only attended in order to continue the row they'd started.

He greeted her sisters first, watching her from the

corner of his eye. She stood very still. If her chin went up any higher, she'd fall over backward.

"Miss Faraday," he said, bowing and turning to her at last. "I'm delighted you decided to attend." He was careful, neutral. Did she wish to pretend the debacle in the mill house had never happened or continue, gloves off, to elaborate on any points of his foul character she'd forgotten to mention at the time?

To his surprise, she merely gave him a weak smile. "Thank you very much for inviting us," she said. She half turned, as though she were going to walk right back up the hill and go home.

Illogically, instead of reviewing clever rebuttals to any barbs she might choose to aim, his mind took him back to the Yule log outing and that utterly inexplicable kiss. Madwoman. She'd made it clear, oh, explicitly clear, that she detested him. Why the devil had she gone and done something like kiss him?

If it had been done to put him off his guard, it had certainly done that. She'd been sweetly inexperienced, but determined all the same. A bizarrely alluring combination. Good God, but he was gawping at her like a schoolboy.

He led the sisters to the disgruntled Miss Eggart and allowed everyone to express their feigned delight at seeing each other again.

"Lord Harrow, you're so good to have invited me," Frederica confided, slipping her mittened hand into his. "You knew it was my Christmas wish! And you know my Christmas wishes always come true."

"Of course," he grinned. "I specialize in Christmas wishes. Are you pleased?" He gestured across the frozen pond.

His aunt really had done a lovely job. She had placed

evergreen-decked torches all around the perimeter of the small lake. They lit the ice with ruddy smudges of gold. Beside them at the bank, tables of holiday fare had been set up, and benches provided seating for those who needed a rest. Already couples were skating together to the music provided by the large amorphous lumps of wool that contained musicians.

Aunt Alva herself was busy directing a flock of white-liveried footmen out onto the ice. Their trays of steaming punch left trails of vapor in the air.

Frederica gave a satisfied squeak and sat down to put on her skates.

"Wassail?" he suggested brightly to the group.

Olivia gave him the Look of Death.

"Yes, please," Frederica said and clapped her hands.

"Not you, Freddie," he said sternly. "Can't run the risk of you getting tipsy. Your family has a reputation for not being able to hold their liquor. But you will skate with me later?"

"Yes, of course. Are those mincemeat pies over there? Oh, but this is grand. You even have Chinese lanterns! It's so beautiful. Just like a scene from a play.

"Look, there is Mr. Thompson. Doesn't he think he's grown up? I beat him last year in the Littleton skating competition. Oh, but he was purple in the face about that. I can beat him again now, just to show him he isn't so grand, dressed up or not."

Jack busied himself by claiming a footman and handing around hot drinks to his guests. He looked around to see that Mrs. Clarke and Miss Eggart had set aside their differences, combined forces, and executed a perfect Wellingtonian pincer movement to entrap the hapless Lord Pennyworth between them. The boy looked somewhat overwhelmed at his good fortune.

Olivia still stood on the bank. She looked so vulnerable there in the flickering torchlight.

He turned away quickly. It was a good thing she'd so brutally put to rest that mad idea of marriage. He'd obviously had a moment of insanity. He tried to summon up the same feeling of relief he'd felt when Miss D'Ore had called off their engagement. Dodged the parson's mousetrap again.

There was too much cinnamon in the mulled wine. It was making his stomach feel queasy.

"I am glad that you decided to come after all," he said to Olivia. "And is Mrs. Smythies looking after the boys and your father? I hope her presence will allow you to enjoy your evening without worry."

Yes, that was all right. Just the kind of thing he would say to anyone.

She looked up at him, and he was shocked to see a defeated expression in her eyes. "Thank you," she said. "I came to show you I was not going to be a martyr." The chin was up again.

Her eyes roved the crowd, taking in his aunt's fantastic decorations, the fir boughs, the gold ribbons entwined around every possible object. All around them, guests were arriving in a flurry of fur wraps and bright wools. They squealed their delight to Aunt Alva as though she was the first person in the world to have conceived of a holiday evening skating party.

Olivia stood in silence, her hands clasped together. He could see that her gloves had been carefully mended where the seams had given way. He felt a strange pinch, the kind of urgent longing one might feel if one saw a lost little kitten. A kitten that would savage you if you dared come too close.

"And I came because I hadn't been to a skating party in such a long time," she said at last.

He genuinely disliked cinnamon. It was wreaking havoc with his insides. He drank the rest of the glass just to distract himself from the ache he felt.

He should greet the rest of the guests. He should go and make certain the servants knew what to do. He should do something other than stand there, doltish, staring at Olivia Faraday, his stomach feeling peculiar.

He shot a glance at his sister, who was speeding by on her husband's arm, whooping with mirth. He half expected her to look his way, see his expression, and burst into howling laughter.

"Well, I suppose since you're here you'd better skate," he said to Olivia with a shrug. He looked around, unsure what to do next. "I suppose you'd better skate with me."

"Very well," she said, looking as though she just needed to nip off to the guillotine first.

Amelia's eyes nearly dropped out of her head when she saw him leading Olivia onto the ice. The minx had the bad grace to drag her husband over and join them. "Hunter," she said, "have you met Miss Faraday? She was with us at the Yule log outing, but I believe she was in the other sled."

Jack's brother-in-law bowed over Olivia's hand, with his usual calm grace. "Yes, I believe we met several years ago in London. Your sister presented you, I believe. We attended a ball given by Mrs. Clarke at her house on Clarges Street."

Trust Westhaven to do the pretty perfectly.

"You were there, Jack, do you remember?" the man went on. "Though I believe you spent most of your time in the card room. Please convey my condolences to your sister, Miss Faraday. I was sorry to hear of her husband's death."

Damn Westhaven. The man remembered everything. And how could he himself have forgotten a meeting with Olivia? He racked his brains, but could come up with no more than a hazy recollection of yet another party where he'd rolled his eyes, played cards for a bit, then taken himself off to gamble in greener pastures.

Good Lord. No wonder Olivia hated him.

"Yes," Amelia said wickedly. "Jack never dances at balls. And he never used to skate, either."

Whatever Olivia thought of this she didn't comment, and at that point the music started up again.

"Shall we skate?" he asked Olivia. She nodded and they set off. It would likely have been entirely acceptable if he had offered his arm to her, or even put a hand on her waist to ensure her safety. He decided not to press his luck.

Olivia Faraday was a good skater, like all country girls. She didn't falter and pretend to stumble like Miss Eggart had, angling for his aid. But, he noted, she didn't put the width of the pond between them, either. She merely skated beside him, silent.

Next to them, Amelia and Hunter kept pace, pretending to comment on the beauty of the winter evening. They maintained carefully neutral expressions, though he could see Amelia was biting her lip and going pink with suppressed merriment. Even Westhaven looked mildly amused.

Olivia, however, looked as though this were just another duty she must do with determination and efficiency.

"How will you celebrate Christmas, Miss Faraday?" he asked.

She put on a little smile, as though she was aware that it was social convention, but wasn't quite used to it. "We will have a quiet holiday. We will merely enjoy having the family together."

"I'm certain your nephews are excited."

"They are. It is all they can talk about. I'm afraid they will be vastly disappointed with their presents of a few gingerbread soldiers, a pair of cockhorses, practical woolen stockings, and the cannon Frederica made for them out of thread spools."

They rounded the edge of the pond, leisurely in stride. He looked around at the white landscape, its contours softened in snow. It must be lovely in summer. Perhaps they would have boating parties, or even a bit of swimming. Then he reminded himself that he was going back to London as soon as possible.

"They are perfect gifts," he said. "Except for the stockings, which are never appreciated as they should be. Have you included cavalry in your baking program?"

She smiled now, a genuine smile. "Of course. And lancers and grenadiers as well. I should have been deemed a very poor aunt if I had been so remiss as to forget them."

He felt a strange pang of loss. He hadn't really intended to offer for her at the mill. He should be relieved that she'd spared him from yet another botched engagement to the wrong woman. But somehow, he found he was wishing yet again she'd accidentally said yes.

"A gingerbread army is absolutely inspired," he said. "Far better than tin. After all, you may have the pleasure of biting their limbs off to simulate injuries."

Merely to torture himself, he looked down at her. She smiled at him, but her eyes looked tired and hollow. Even in the torchlight, he could see that she appeared quite drawn. "Are you all right, Miss Faraday? I would hate to tire you out with too much skating."

Ordinarily, Olivia would have put a flea in his ear for treating her like a weakling. Instead she merely looked away. "Yes. Perhaps we should go back to the bank. I'm a little tired. I suppose I'm not feeling myself today."

He considered making a joke about her continuing to suffer from the aftereffects of wassail consumption, but decided he preferred to live.

A chilly glare from his aunt reminded him of his duties, so he guided Olivia to the benches set at the bank and introduced her to a group of young ladies and gentlemen warming themselves over cups of punch and hot mince pies. He found himself rather annoyed to hear the men eagerly pounce on her, offering her refreshment and making her laugh with their witty sallies.

"What in heaven's name is making you frown like that?" his aunt demanded when he reached her. "I really do wish you'd make more of an effort, Jack. This is my first skating outing in years and you will frighten everyone off by looking as though you're detesting every moment of it."

"Not in the least," he lied. "What can I do for you?"

"Well," she smoothed her gloves and settled her fur cap more firmly on her head. "Primarily I wished to remind you that we have some very important guests here."

He looked at her blankly for a moment, then realized that this was meant to hint that he should not be spending his time entertaining someone his aunt regarded as little more than the groundskeeper's daughter.

"Miss Berrywell will need to be skated with. I hear she will be going down to London in the spring," the dowager continued. "Very old family, you know. Very well-to-do. And, of course, Lady Shropshire. She asked after you specifically. You might consider one of the Hebb sisters. Their mother was a Granville. And there is always Miss Eggart. She has been spending a great deal of time with Lord Pennyworth of late. I do think you should step in and do something. After all, you met her first."

"And therefore I have called dibs on her?" he asked. "Nonsense. A sensible woman would choose Pennyworth over me any day. I applaud her taste."

His aunt scowled. "You take things a great deal too lightly. I would have thought she would have been a perfect match for you."

Because she was fashionable and foolish and didn't have an unselfish thought in her head, he added mentally. Just like himself.

Across the pond he saw Susanna Clarke playfully trying to lure Lord Ballyglen under a kissing bough hung from a branch. That gentleman appeared more embarrassed than interested. He rolled his eyes, made a comment behind his hand to his friends, and then turned away, laughing. Even in the darkness Jack could see that Mrs. Clarke had gone an unattractive shade of red.

Jack drew a breath, bowed to his aunt, and went to her.

"Why, hello, Lord Harrow," Susanna said, making a rallying attempt to recover her countenance. "What great foolishness is always to be found at skating parties."

"Indeed," he said. "I hope you are enjoying yourself." What was he supposed to do now? It was obvious that Mrs. Clarke was on the prowl. If he didn't introduce her quickly to some eligible man she would certainly start in with him again. "Have you met Mr. Fitzgerald?"

He congratulated himself on the stroke of genius. Fitzgerald was young, handsome, and single. What else could the lady wish for?

"Third son," she said scornfully. "Poor as a church mouse. He'd never do." She looked across the pond, her eyes searching for someone.

"I see Lord Randolf has arrived."

"Randolf," she said with an expression of scorn much like her sister's. "I detest him more than anyone. I've never met a man more cold. It's almost sinister."

She gave a dramatic shudder, her eyes lingering on the man. "Never mind about me. I know what everyone thinks. And I don't care. I can take care of myself." She interrupted his protests. "Now go and skate with some of the other girls like a good boy. I am going to talk to Lord Axeram."

He allowed himself to be waved away, telling himself that he didn't give a hang how the Faradays resolved their troubles. It wasn't his fault that their father was dotty. Still, he'd stayed up half the night working out how he could pension the man off in a way that Olivia wouldn't see as charity.

Though by jingo, Olivia shouldn't be so proud. Or stubborn, more like. Why couldn't she just take things that were offered to her like a sensible person? He'd met with the solicitor about the annuity. At least that was something. And had written a crony at Eton to see if something could be done for the boys. He mentally ticked off the list of Olivia's worries. They could live in modest gentility on what he would settle on them.

But even so, he knew that money, while it was certainly a worry, wasn't really the point.

He still felt an uncomfortable ache, so he steered

clear of the cinnamon-laced mulled wine and helped himself to a plain glass of port.

He noticed Lord Randolf standing across the table, out of range of the flickering light of the torches. He was looking out across the pond with an expression of removed disinterest.

"Very pleasant gathering, Harrow," he said quietly. He took a sniff of the punch he held and set the cup down with a look of distaste. "Have you escaped Mrs. Clarke's clutches?"

The man had deigned to attend, but he had not worn skates. A condescending sign to be sure. Instead he merely stood on the bank, determined to be unamused.

Jack felt the hairs at the back of his neck prickle. He agreed with Mrs. Clarke's assessment that the man was cold. It was a little unnerving. "I'm not certain what you mean," he said, offering the man a glass of wine to replace the punch.

"She throws herself at any man with a title. Plans to be engaged again by the new year." He raised a lorgnette and gave the woman a cool stare. Happily, she appeared too involved in her flirtation with Lord Axeram to notice. As they watched, Olivia skated over to the pair, wearing her fiercest frown.

Jack's tendons tightened. Randolf, snobbish dog, was walking close to the line. After all, the Faradays were under his protection, in a manner of speaking. And a gentleman shouldn't speak that way of anyone.

To his surprise, the man gave a dry laugh and smiled. "You'd like to tap my claret, I don't doubt it. You look game enough to take on a battalion. I don't blame you, either. Perhaps it will make you feel slightly mollified to know that it is only what is vulgarly known as sour grapes."

"I beg your pardon?"

The man's lips narrowed in an expression of disgust. "I'm in love with the woman."

He couldn't mean Olivia. He'd been so obviously courting her sister. Still, Jack felt the need to be absolutely positive. "Mrs. Clarke?"

"Indeed." Again the humorless laugh. "And the woman showed the unexpected good sense to send me packing when I offered a . . . less than traditional arrangement." Randolf exhaled a long, white breath and then took a sip of wine, his lids half closed over his dark eyes. "One would have thought—"

"That she was desperate enough?" Jack filled in, trying to control his rising annoyance.

Randolf's eyes met his. "Indeed. But you will be delighted to know that she was not amenable to the suggestion. Decisively." He turned to scan the crowd again. "Now, you may call me out with an even greater sense of purpose, if you please."

Jack drew a deep breath and slowly let it out. "I think you will do a much better job of punishing yourself than I ever would." He thought for a moment. As though *he* would ever be able to offer helpful advice where women were concerned. "Perhaps if you—"

"No," the man cut him off. "It is well and truly done now."

Jack was about to offer more. Sympathy, advice, he wasn't certain. But at that moment his eyes drifted back to the Faraday sisters. They had been joined at the bank by a young gentleman.

Mr. North. Will North's estate manager cousin. The man to whom he had offered Mr. Faraday's position.

In a moment Jack had skidded up to the group with unseemly haste, a spray of ice dusting their clothes. He felt as though he was watching a fuse disappear into a powder keg.

Frederica, wearing her most grown-up face, was introducing North around as her new acquaintance. Everyone paused and looked slightly surprised at Jack's dramatic appearance, but he could only stand there, unable to stop what was about to happen.

After a moment of watching Jack gape like a fish, Olivia turned back to North. "And what brings you to Littleton, sir?" she asked.

Jack flinched, waiting for the explosion.

North looked at him and smiled an easy, innocent, hopelessly naïve smile exactly like his cousin Willie's. "Lord Harrow, ma'am," he replied happily. "He has made me his new estate manager."

The explosion manifested itself in silence.

"Estate manager," Olivia echoed at last in a voice barely above a whisper. "I wasn't aware the position was open."

"Indeed, neither was I. But Lord Harrow wrote and— I hope you'll forgive me interrupting your skating party, my lord. I know it isn't the thing. But I just arrived at the house, and they said you were down here. I wanted to come and thank you right away. I know you did it as a favor to my cousin." The man turned back to Olivia, positively gleaming with fresh-faced delight. "Lord Harrow is the most generous of men."

Jack wanted to drop through the ice into the freezing water below. "You didn't get my second letter?" he asked, knowing what the answer would be.

North shook his head. "I came straight from Surrey. It took a while, since I had to take rides on wagons and carts, and walk when I couldn't find either."

Jack resisted the violent urge to clench his hands in

his hair and shout self-directed curses. He hadn't even remembered to send the man coach money. No, he'd blithely given away the position without even considering how North would get himself here, what he would do once he got here, or even if he would be suitable for the position.

And of course he hadn't given a flirting thought to what he would do if he hadn't exactly gotten around to officially discharging Mr. Faraday when North arrived. Frankly, after he'd written the rather embarrassing letter reneging his offer several days ago, he'd sent it off and promptly forgotten he'd invited North to take the position in the first place. It was horribly, excruciatingly, humiliatingly typical.

"There's been a mistake," he said, his voice sounding rushed.

He'd find something else for North. It wouldn't mean much loss of face. The man only wanted a chance to prove himself at something.

North's face fell. "A mistake?"

"No," Olivia said quickly. "There hasn't been a mistake."

"Olivia . . ."

She took Mr. North's hand and shook it. "Congratulations, Mr. North. Littleton is a lovely estate. I think you will find it a great joy to manage. Now please, if you will excuse me."

With a smile that looked natural except for the slight tremble at the corners, she turned on her skates and disappeared into the crowd.

Sixteen

Olivia took off her skates, walked up the hill, down the lane, and somehow found that she had continued walking until she was nearly home. How ridiculous she must look, stalking along the dirty country road in the dark, her skates flopping over her shoulder, bumping bruises with each stride.

She should feel angry, perhaps, but somehow she did not. She had been shocked at first, of course, but instead of feeling betrayed at finding that Lord Harrow had replaced her father, she only felt a strange sense of calm. Perhaps it was the relief of defeat.

She had worked so hard, concentrated solely on getting Harrow to believe that her father was capable of continuing his duties as agricultural consultant. Now she could see that it had been a hopeless task all along. Did she really think no one would see that her father was lost in a fog of dreams?

She herself was likely the only one who hadn't seen the obvious. And it was comforting, in a strange way, to know that Mr. North had the position. How just like Harrow to offer it. He'd trusted his friend that the young man was competent. Despite North's lack of experience, she had no doubt that the man would be good at his work. He seemed earnest, honest. He only needed a chance.

She wrapped her arms around herself and wished that her half-boots had more substantial soles. The chill of the frosty ground was creeping up her legs.

She felt a bit silly, leaving the skating party so precipitously. Frederica and Susanna had both looked at her as though she'd lost her mind. But she'd needed a bit of time alone to think.

At least it was a lovely night to walk, despite the cold. The moon was full, and its light on the snow lit up the countryside almost as bright as day. It was beautiful. The shadows cast by the moon were sharp and black, like whitework cutouts in fanciful patterns. There was only the merest breath of wind to break the still silence of the evening. Her jumbled thoughts seemed out of place in the serenity.

It all came back to one thing. If she had said yes to Harrow's proposal, things would have been different. She sighed a cloud of vapor. Very different.

Perhaps they could go and live with Aunt Sarah in Wales. They would manage. The boys would have to rely on herself for schooling, but she'd had a good governess in her time. She would do her best. And perhaps someday a man like Harrow would give them a chance, just as he'd done for Mr. North.

As she neared the house, she noticed that there was a smell in the air, like a faulty chimney, only worse. Had the boys put something up the flue again? She quickened her step.

As she came in the door, it was obvious that something had gone spectacularly wrong. A low cloud of eye-watering smoke hung in the hallway, and the stench of something scorched made it difficult to breathe.

Mrs. Smythies staggered down the stairs. The

woman's shawl was half off her shoulders; her hair was in disarray and her face flushed and sooty.

"What has happened?" Olivia demanded, panic rising in her throat.

"Miss! It weren't my fault. I dozed off for just a minute, it being late, and your pa decided to light a pipe in bed. Dotty old man, he is. Didn't know what was what. The fire's out but you're lucky the whole place didn't go up like a tinderbox."

"Is my father hurt?"

The woman dragged her sleeve across her face and then looked at the black mark it left from wrist to elbow. "He's fair enough. Swore at me like a sailor, though."

"I should think so," Olivia snapped. She pushed past the woman and raced up the stairs. Blue smoke filled the hallway, choking her. She could hear George and Teddy crying and her father's voice calling querulously for her from where they had gathered in her bedroom.

"Papa," she ran to him. "Are you all right?" She saw the singed edges of his dressing gown and checked him for injuries.

He pulled away from her. "Of course I'm all right. Stop fussing over me, girl. And get these brats out of here. The noise is unbearable."

The boys clung to her, sobbing out their disjointed version of the story.

"We were going down to the kitchen because Georgie wanted a piece of pie and we heard that old lady screaming and so we went into the room and there was a fire on the bed curtains and the lady was shouting and beating it with a pillow and the fire went out, but the room's all ruined. What will we do, Aunt 'Livia?"

"Stop all this screeching," her father said irritably. "I don't understand what is going on. That woman was a banshee. Why did you bring her here? She nearly pulled my arm out of its . . . its . . . well, she right wrenched me getting me out of bed. I don't like that."

"What were you thinking, Papa? A pipe in bed?"

He looked like a guilty, frightened child for a moment. "I couldn't find my tobacco," he said. He pulled himself up and shuffled over to the window. Olivia could see that he was agitated. "I finally found it in my pillowcase. Boys must have hidden it. People are always hiding my things. When I saw it, I decided I would have a good pipe."

She refrained from chastising him. The damage was already done, and there wasn't any point in upsetting any of them further. She quieted the boys, and once their fear had diminished into a curiosity to see the scene of the disaster, she allowed them to lead her into Papa's room to examine the damage.

Mrs. Smythies had opened the windows to let out the smoke. It was freezing. The bed was a mass of charred feathers and fabric. Clumps of half-burnt feathers blew around in eddies in the faint breeze. The curtains rhythmically bellied out into the room and then were sucked back against the casements.

"That lady said that Grandpapa could have been roasted alive," George said, picking a bubble of plaster on the ruined wall.

Olivia pulled him away and looked up at the blackened ceiling. "At least no one was hurt."

"She said Grandpapa was a crazy old man who would get us all killed."

She smiled sadly at her nephew. He would never know the man her father had been. "Of course not. This was just an accident."

Harrow had been right. Her father was never going to

be himself. She'd known it for longer than she cared to admit but the shock of seeing such ugly evidence of it was painful.

They looked around a little more to ascertain that the fire truly was out. The boys were complaining of the smell, and there was little else to be done, so she escorted them out and closed the door.

Poor Mr. North would inherit one slightly damaged estate manager's cottage, to be sure. Ah, well. At least the estate itself was in order. What was one scorched room when it came to that?

Mrs. Smythies stood at the top of the stairs. Her rheumy eyes were wild in her dirty face. "It weren't my fault, miss. I know they'll say I was tippling but I wasn't. I wasn't at all. At least not but a drop on account of the cold. I didn't know I would be watching after someone dangerous-like! Keep an eye on him, Lord Harrow said. He didn't say he'd be likely to burn us all up! He should have told me. He should have told me."

"It's all right, Mrs. Smythies," Olivia said tiredly. "You did the right thing. And I know if you were not here, we might have indeed had a far larger disaster on our hands. I'm glad you had the foresight to take care of the fire efficiently. You're welcome to go home now. I realize it is late."

The woman looked at her with an expression of bewilderment. She obviously expected the blame to be laid on her head. After a moment, she bobbed a quick curtsey and went down the stairs, her wooden heels clopping on each step as she went. Olivia heard her muttering to herself as she dragged on her coat, and then the back door banged shut. In her father's bedroom, Olivia could hear the windows rattling. In her own, her nephews were quarreling over the role each had played in the heroic rescue. The rest of the house was strangely silent.

The heavy feeling within her grew slightly more weighty. It seemed as though things would never be right again.

At the top of the stairs hung a bunch of holly Susanna had collected. She'd complained that the house was dismal without Christmas decorations, but somehow this one bedraggled bough tied with a wrinkled, red-velvet ribbon made the rest of the house seem all the more drab. The glossy leaves hung on the newel post, in the place where they had always put something at every Christmas season, on every newel post, in every house they lived in. Olivia was surprised that her sister would remember it.

Thoughts of past holidays brought back memories of Christopher. He would not be home this Christmas. Strange how she had somehow, in the back of her mind, been waiting for him. Since he'd left for Spain, she had been focused entirely on ensuring their future, on building something she could hand over to Christopher when he returned. And when he returned she would be free to start her life again.

She sat down on the stairs, her feet suddenly as weary as her mind.

Christopher would not be coming back. There would be no one to shoulder the running of the household. She hadn't wanted to believe things had changed. But of course they had. She would have to stop living in this strange purgatory and move on.

She took the velvet ribbon tying the bunch of holly and rubbed the comfort of its furry bloom against her fingers.

It was time to face many ugly realities. Christopher

was dead. Her father would never be himself again. The position at Littleton Park was lost. And Lord Jack Harrow was nothing but a pleasant dream.

But she couldn't just sit here and tot up her losses. They would manage. It wouldn't be as they planned, but she would think of something. It wasn't the end of the world. But somehow she found that she was crying anyway.

Seventeen

Jack dismounted his horse in front of the Faradays' cottage. Willard was engaged in his perpetual maintenance, today making certain that the flowerbeds were well covered with straw to protect them from the frost. His impossibly meticulous habits must have come from long association with Mr. Faraday. The manservant looked up and touched his forelock.

"Working, Willard?" Jack asked. "Miss Faraday is far too strict a mistress if she has you working on the day before Christmas." He was pleased to find that the jovial comment came out easily. His voice hardly stumbled over her name at all.

"No, sir," Willard grinned. "Woke up in a sweat last night about these roses. It's been colder than I thought it would be. And there's been a bit of wind, you know. Mr. Faraday always likes to have everything right and tight in the garden, and the bedding in the wintertime can make all the difference."

Jack nodded. Olivia often said the same thing about the fields. He cast a glance at the house, suddenly feeling rather cowardly. After last night, his gorgon would do away with him with a glance. "How is Mr. Faraday?"

"I reckon you heard about last night, then?" Willard said, his lined face dropping into sober creases. "We had a scare, we did. It was a pity it was Molly's night off. She feels right bad she wasn't here to take care of things. Feels she shouldn't have taken the night when she knew the Misses Faraday and Mrs. Clarke would be out." The man leaned on his pitchfork. He'd become a great deal friendlier to Jack over the course of their rambles with Miss Faraday.

"We all knew Mrs. Smythies was a bit of a tippler. Molly told Miss Faraday straight out that she should send the woman off same as last time. But Miss Faraday said no, that you'd sent the woman, and we should all take our nights out as planned."

Jack squinted back up at the house. A black tongue of smoke marred the whitewashed front above one of the upstairs windows. He suppressed a feeling of sickness. This was all his fault. He hadn't looked into Mrs. Smythies' credentials enough. He hadn't considered that two small boys and an old man might wreak havoc in a few evening hours.

This is what he got for attempting to play the grown-up, he mused. Old care-for-nobody Jack Harrow would never have gotten himself into this tangle. And if he had, he would have hared off and let someone else deal with the consequences. Good old Jack Harrow.

He drew a breath, and decided to get on with it. Time to suffer the results of his actions, regardless of how well intended. He looked back and saw the workmen's cart was coming down the lane. It had been a piece of work to get them on the day of Christmas Eve, but he'd wheedled and cajoled them. After all, there'd be plenty more opportunities to hire them if he followed through with even half of Faraday's plans for the estate.

He bid Willard good day and went to knock on the door. To his surprise, it was Olivia herself who answered it. It was clear that he'd interrupted something. Her face was covered with a dusting of flour. She'd obviously attempted to remove it with a corner of the apron tied at her slim waist, but the powder still dusted the edge of her jaw, the fine hair at her temples, the tender flesh behind her ears.

"I came to call and see if you were all well, after last night," he said, his voice coming out explosively gruff.

"Thank you," she said, giving her face another ineffective scrub. "We had a bit of a scare, but everyone is well." As if in afterthought, she forced the ends of her mouth up into a tired smile. These days, though, the cold glare was tempered with a new patina of sadness. It no longer intimidated him. Instead he found he would much rather take her into his arms and whisper unspeakably sentimental nonsense. Of course, he knew better.

"Harrow!" Frederica came running down the hallway, her freckled face flushed. "Did you hear what happened? You should see Papa's room. I burst into tears when I saw it. Papa could have been innodated."

"Immolated," Olivia corrected her automatically. Then she shook herself. "That isn't so, Frederica. There is no need to be so dramatic. It was only an accident and Papa is safe."

She could not very well slam the door on him at this point, so she had no choice but to invite him in. "Frederica," she said, not meeting Jack's eyes, "why don't you take Lord Harrow to see Papa?"

"Miss Faraday," he said, catching Olivia's wrist before she could disappear back into the kitchen. Her bones were so tiny. He loosened his grip, afraid he might break her. Beneath his fingers he could feel her warmth, her pulse, the strength of her muscles straining to pull away from him. He released her and watched her cross her arms. She didn't move away, though, but looked up at him with an expression of pain.

"Yes? What do you want?" She tried to say it with her old shrewishness, but he could tell she was tired.

He had already told her once before what he wanted, and she'd rejected it. This was obviously not an invitation to revisit the subject. "I have taken the liberty of hiring several workmen to come here to assess and begin repairing the damage to your house."

She paused, the hand holding the corner of her apron tightening.

"That is very kind." Her voice was neutral. "But, of course, it is your house. You must do with it as you please."

He resisted the urge to roll his eyes. Trying to take care of an independent woman like Olivia was like juggling knives: difficult, dangerous, and utterly, utterly useless. It would have been a great deal more satisfying if she had thrown herself into his arms and exclaimed that he'd just won her eternal devotion. But no, then it wouldn't be like Olivia. And then he wouldn't be so dashed in love with her.

But Frederica was pulling him toward her father's room, and he could hear Mrs. Clarke's children starting to quarrel in the kitchen, so he pushed all those urges aside, drew a deep breath, and followed Olivia's sister into the oven that was Mr. Faraday's study.

There was nothing to be done. Olivia collapsed into a worn chair in the drawing room and looked about her. The workmen were busy upstairs, Papa was talking with

Freddie and Harrow, and Susanna, well, Lord knew where she was.

Unlike her usual habit of staying abed until noon, her sister had gotten up at the crack of dawn and left the house. Doubtless it was some romantic assignation that would evaporate when the hapless young man discovered that Susanna was hell-bent on getting engaged before the new year.

Olivia sighed. Nothing she'd said would convince Susanna that marriage wasn't the only option for the future. She only hoped her sister had the sense not to get herself ruined. That was all the family needed—scandal on top of it all.

She felt strangely restless. For the first time in at least a year, there was nothing that required her attention. She'd spent the morning baking the last batch of gingerbread infantrymen. She'd wrapped her little presents for her family and hidden them away where Freddie couldn't find them before tomorrow morning. She'd spoken to the workmen, and Molly had promised that she and Susanna would spend the afternoon cleaning up Papa's room as best possible, once the men had gone. Happily, it seemed that the damage was not so bad as they'd originally thought.

Oh yes, Olivia had assured the household, everything was fine. Though, of course, everything was not fine. But that could wait until after Christmas.

She picked up another piece of greenery and tied it to the last with black thread. Whatever was to come, they would have a proper Christmas. The presents would be meager enough, but they would have to do.

She had watched Frederica embroider handkerchiefs with Susanna's initials and knew that her younger sister had discovered the hiding place of the coral bracelet

Susanna intended to give her. Susanna's twins had revealed at dinner last night that they meant to present their mama with a drawing of England they'd been working on in the schoolroom and Susanna had borrowed Olivia's pin money to buy a rather splendid fob for Papa's watch.

Olivia smiled and twisted a bit of ribbon around the garland. Hardly lavish, or even original, presents. At least they were all together.

"Are you pleased with the work of the men?"

She looked up and saw Lord Harrow in the doorway. She dropped her eyes quickly to the garland in her lap. To her annoyance, she saw that her fingers were trembling. She forced them to keep working. "Yes. They seem to think that the damage is not irreparable."

"Devil take it, but this room is always freezing," he exclaimed, rubbing his hands together. "Your house is always either baking or freezing. Look, I've hired a proper nurse from the village. She will come in for the afternoons next week, and then come to live here permanently after the New Year. I realize that leaves a burden on you for a while longer, but I didn't feel I could ask the woman to leave her family at Christmastime." He crossed his arms over his chest, scowling. "I've sent over a goose as well. And a few things from the hothouse. For your father. I know he likes oranges."

She felt her jaw grow painfully tight, but she kept her eyes focused on her work. "There is no need to do these things to assuage your guilt, Lord Harrow. I assure you, I do not blame you for the fire."

To her dismay, he came further into the room and sat down in the chair beside her. "You should. You told me that Mrs. Smythies was not the most reliable of women."

"She saved my father's life."

"She also endangered it." He took up one end of the garland, examining the prickly fir boughs as though he'd never seen anything like it before. "I want to do right by your family, Olivia," he said in a low voice.

The gentleness of his tone made unwanted tears start in her eyes. She should hate him. He'd taken her father's livelihood. He'd made it impossible for them to go on as they had been. He had changed everything.

She took another piece of greenery but dropped it in her clumsiness. He took it up and held it out to her.

"We appreciate your kindness, but I must assure you that it isn't necessary," she said, taking the bit of evergreen so quickly that it scratched her. "We don't need someone to take care of us, Lord Harrow. We are not a Christmas charity case. There are many other poor families in the neighborhood who would benefit more from your—" His hand closed over hers and her voice died in her throat.

"I'm not doing it out of charity," he said.

"Generosity sprung from guilt is much the same as charity," she countered.

He released her hand, as though it had merely been a pleasantry to take it in the first place. "I do feel guilty," he admitted. "And I know you do as well. We should have known not to leave your father alone. But that is not why I sent you things. I care about your family, Olivia."

Yes, of course. He cared about her family. Papa, Frederica, Susanna, he cared about them. That's why he was kind. She'd done everything cold and rude in her power to ensure he couldn't care about *her*, now hadn't she? She'd even humiliated him by turning down his proposal. And still he was kind.

She stood up abruptly. "Well! This garland is done. I shall have to put it on the banister. Or perhaps on the mantel here. There is such a great fuss made over the holidays, don't you think?"

"I had written Mr. North, you know," he said, standing up and crossing to the window, "to tell him that the position was not available."

"I guessed as much. But I am glad the letter didn't reach him. He will be a good estate manager."

"Not as good as your father."

She smiled and tucked the garland behind the ornaments on the mantel. There was a vase her mother had painted, the miniature of Christopher in his regimentals, the pair of silhouettes Susanna had sent of the boys when they were infants. "We never lived anywhere more than a few years," she said with a shrug. "My father's whole career was to design things. Set things to right. He worked his magic on the greatest estates in England. Then he would move on." She looked over her shoulder at him. "It is time for us to move on."

It was true. She'd become too attached to things the way they were. But things must always change, and she would weather this, this heartbreak, the way she'd weathered everything else.

Behind her she heard him move from the window, but she did not turn around. "The house is yours, Olivia," he said quietly. "I gave your father the deed a few minutes ago."

She drew a sharp breath; her heart suddenly felt all edges, painful in her chest. "I only wanted my father to have the position because I thought it would bring him back. But no one can do that. Your kindness to my family goes beyond the bounds of propriety." She could hear the old bitterness back in her tone.

He drew several breaths before he answered. "I am trying, for the first time in my life, to be responsible. You will accuse me of throwing money at my problems, I know. But it is the only thing I know to do. I cannot take care of people like you do. I can only pay for some of their worries to go away."

She kept her back to him, but she could feel that he was close behind her. "I cannot take care of people," she countered. "I have been able to do nothing for my family."

He reached over her shoulder and touched her cheek. She flinched, but could not move away. "You have flour on your face," he said softly.

She scrubbed at her jaw. "I was playing at bullet pudding with Susanna's boys." She had thought he would never touch her again. And when he had, so innocently, it had brought back a painful flood of memories.

"The game where you root about with your face in a dish of flour looking for a bean?" He laughed. "I should have liked to have seen that."

She felt her face growing warm. She pushed him aside to get toward the mirror above the mantelpiece. She should say something. Something witty and flirtatious. She should put on her Susanna face and let him know that her feelings . . . well, her feelings had changed. She merely continued to rub at her face until it was unattractively flushed.

"You take care of your family very well," he said gravely. "And they deserve every kindness." He did not seem to notice that they still stood very close. If she'd been Susanna, she would have found a way to entice him to embrace her. If she'd been Frederica she would have thrown her arms around him. Instead, she only stood there, aching.

His smile twisted into an expression of sadness mixed with hope. "Tell me you will not fling it all back in my face. Frederica has developed quite a *tendre* for the goose."

"Jack," she said. Then, realizing what had come out of her mouth— "Lord Harrow, I mean. We cannot accept these gifts. It is entirely inappropriate. People will talk."

"I've let it be known that these were all things that my late uncle requested be done in his will. You needn't worry that people will think I gave you undue attention."

At the moment she would gladly suffer a little undue attention.

"I know you think I will renew my suit," he said, obviously mistaking the meaning of her protesting stammers. "You have made it very clear to me that it is not what you wish. Please do not let what I've done make you think that I wish anything from you in return."

"I do," she blurted out.

He looked taken aback. "I assure you, Miss Faraday—"

"No, I mean I do want you to renew your suit." Good God, had she no more finesse than that? Very well. It was out. Her heart was suddenly pounding painfully and fast. An uncomfortable sweat started out at the back of her neck.

She watched his face go carefully blank. The clock seemed to be ticking unreasonably loudly in the silent room.

Then he drew a quick breath and gave a boyish laugh. "I can't credit that, I'm afraid. It would be a great deal too easy if I could merely change your mind by sending over a few paltry gifts." He smiled, but it did not reach his eyes. "And you should have grossly overpaid. Perhaps you have developed a sudden, burning desire to become a viscountess, but surely you would agree that life as my wife would hardly be worth that sacrifice. Your sister would counsel you to aim much higher."

He thought she wanted to marry him for the money. "It isn't because of your decision regarding my father," she said desperately. "It has nothing to do with that. I know you cannot keep him on. Maybe you feel differently now that he is unemployed, but please, my feelings have nothing to do with your position or fortune—" Good heavens, the more she protested, the more untrue it sounded. "Please marry me."

He laughed again, that shy uncomfortable laugh. "Yes, well . . . I've received very flattering proposals from all three Faraday girls." He smiled, but it was weak, as though he really couldn't manage it any longer. "Please assure your sisters that I will do everything I can for your family. That has not changed. But as for the rest—" he looked at her, his eyes troubled, but unreadable. "Well, I believe it is not something that either you or I could truly want."

She stared at him, uncomprehending. He'd rejected her. She'd thrown herself at him, utterly shamelessly, and he'd rejected her. And Susanna and Frederica had done the same? She resisted the urge to crawl under the rug. Instead she drew herself up as tall as she could. She knew he could see the tears that were blurring her vision, but she refused to drop her gaze. "As you wish," she said in a hollow voice.

He pressed his lips together. He looked nothing like the bluff young man she had come to know. His face had the hardened look of a much older man. The laughing expression in his eyes was replaced with one that was somber, even stern.

"There is one thing you could do," he said. "Something you could tolerate for me, in the name of tradition." His eyes lifted up to the mirror above her head. She followed his gaze and saw the kissing bough tied to the ornate scrollwork at the top.

She didn't say yes. She didn't say anything. Perhaps he was giving her the opportunity to reject him as he had rejected her. She didn't care. She merely raised her mouth to his and waited.

He kissed her gently. It was nothing like the kiss they had shared in the woods. This was restrained, careful. But she could feel his hands tighten around her waist and his breath quicken. She wanted him to kiss her deeply and hold her pressed to the length of his body as he had that night. But instead he released her and stepped back.

"There," she said, struggling to recover herself. "There. We are done."

"Thank you, Miss Faraday." He drew a tight breath. "I believe our score is settled." He sketched her a bow. "As you say, we are done."

Eighteen

Jack stepped out of the door and drew a deep breath. The dry winter air was painful in his lungs, but he didn't mind. It helped dispel the fog of that damp, cold room. It shocked the mind out of its reverie, helped keep what had just happened from becoming a memory.

He should be congratulating himself. After all, as Olivia had said, it was done. He'd rather neatly disentangled himself from his obligations to the Faraday family while not arousing any scandal for his favoritism.

"Yes," he said aloud in a voice that seemed, even to himself, to sound falsely cheerful. "And then after Christmas, back to the normal life in London." He strode off down the lane, trying to remember why that should have been appealing.

It was too bright outside. The sun on the snow was painfully reflective. He realized how long it had been since he'd seen a sunny, snowy day in the countryside. He couldn't afford to be sentimental. Dash it all, he was going back to London right away.

"Marry me," he said scornfully, thinking back on Olivia's words. "Now that your father's put to pasture you're not too good for me." He fell silent, uncomfortable with the bitterness of his own tone. He'd actually been tempted to accept her unorthodox proposal.

Well, if truth to be told, he'd been very tempted. But it was obvious that she had only meant to throw herself on the marital pyre for her family. Her cold reaction to his kiss proved that.

He still felt like kicking himself.

"Stop! Wait!"

He turned around and saw Frederica burst out of the house and run to catch him. He realized only as his heart returned to its former place in the pit of his stomach that he'd been hoping that it would be someone else. "Where is your coat, Freddie? You'll freeze to death."

"I only came to thank you," she said, throwing her arms around his neck in an impulsive way that reminded him of his sister Amelia. "You are the kindest man I've ever met." She put her cold little hands in his. "Susanna is too spoilt to notice, and Olivia is too proud to admit it, but your gifts mean a great deal to us. Olivia was planning on having mutton and turnips for our Christmas dinner. And there was little enough of that. Now we shall have goose like the old days! And Molly said you are sending the boys to school and that you have given Papa the deed to the house. It means that we shall not be ruined entirely after all."

She bit her lip and looked slightly cast down for a moment. "Oh, I do wish you would have married me."

He could not help but laugh at her comical expression, but it felt rather painful. Like the time he'd broken a rib in Jackson's boxing salon. "I'm sorry, my dear," he said lightly, "but I think you will find someone who will suit you far better if you wait a little."

Perhaps he would see Frederica again someday, when he was back in London, and she came to make her bow. She would descend on the *ton* like a mortar shell in a fetching bonnet. He tortured himself a little with a vision of Olivia, married and happy, sponsoring her sister's Season. Olivia married to someone else.

He'd made the right decision. The Faraday sisters saw him as a way out. Olivia had refused him when she thought he would reinstate her father, but she begged him to marry her when there was no other option for her family.

The gorgon had begged. That should make him laugh. Instead, he found that he felt like he'd drunk a gallon of that plaguey cinnamon-flavored Christmas punch.

"But everything will be all right now," Frederica was saying. "My Christmas wish came true."

"You wished for a goose?" he teased her.

She looked at him as though he were feebleminded. "A goose! I wished for far more. I mean, if you are going to make a Christmas wish, you might as well make it a really big one."

He unwound his scarf and wrapped it around the girl's neck. The poor creature would catch her death if she kept on chattering. "And how did it come true?" he asked.

She hugged her arms around herself and spun in a circle in the snow. The gesture reminded him of Olivia the night of the Yule log outing. The night he'd kissed her.

"It has all come out even better than I could have wished it. At first, I wished I could marry you and that everything would be all right with the family. But now everything is all right, and I didn't even have to get married. Which is rather a relief as it might have interfered with my plans to travel the world. Instead, it is Susanna who is going to be married, and we shall be related to an earl."

He stared at her. "Susanna is getting married?"

Frederica's face crumpled into an expression of

contrition. "I told her I wouldn't tell anyone. But I didn't think you would count. She didn't want anyone to know just yet—I think because she is not quite sure she is happy with it. Though I can't see why she wouldn't be. After all, he is an earl."

"Lord Randolf?" he asked. Susanna must have reconsidered his suit.

"Yes. She's in her room crying about it now. I don't know what all the fuss is about." She shrugged. "I mean, Lord Randolf is rather old. And he is very stern-looking. A bit like Bluebeard. Though of course he hasn't a beard. And hopefully no dead wives, either. But Susanna shouldn't care for sternness. After all, he shall be able to buy her lovely things."

So Susanna had grasped the brass ring with the most gilding, and now she was unsure if it was what she wanted. Like most other ladies of good breeding, she was raised to be romantic but to act in the interests of her family's fortune and rank.

A sudden thought occurred to him. "Are you certain your sister is going to *marry* Lord Randolf?" he asked. "A proper wedding? In a church?"

Freddie looked nonplussed. "Of course. Do you think my sister is a curtsey-ann?"

"Courtesan," he corrected. "And no. Of course not. Freddie, come back into the house and explain all this to me. Your sister should not have to marry Lord Randolf if she does not wish it."

Frederica raised her chin, in a gesture very like Olivia. "I think she is being very brave. I would have married an earl if I had been able to. I told you it was all your fault for not marrying me. Now Susanna has gone and engaged herself to Lord Randolf, and all to save us from starving to death."

"What are you talking about?" he exclaimed. "I would not have let your family starve to death."

"I know that," she said with an exaggerated roll of her eyes. "But Olivia is so sticky about charity. She wanted to give all your gifts back. Susanna and she had an enormous row again yesterday about marrying for money. And then today Susanna got engaged." She hung back a little as he led her back toward the house. "Does that mean that you will take back all of your gifts? I certainly hope you won't take the goose."

He smiled and resisted the urge to pull her plaits. "No, of course not, Freddie. I wouldn't dream of parting you from your goose."

He didn't want to go back to the house. Too much had just happened there. He was more than a little afraid that he might see Olivia. Dash it all, one look and he would take her up on her ridiculously insincere proposal. But the door to the drawing room was closed now, so he had no choice but to draw a deep breath and plunge into the inferno of the study.

Mr. Faraday was sitting in front of the fire, baking, as always. Jack always half expected the man to be blackened on one side from the heat.

Olivia's father looked up and smiled when he saw Jack enter, apparently unshaken by the fact that he was striding in unannounced barely half an hour after having left.

"Hello, young man," he said pleasantly, though without recognition.

Olivia and her sister were sitting knee to knee on the settee. Their flushed and angry faces showed that the secret was out.

Susanna rose to her feet and gave him a brightly false

smile. "You must congratulate me, Lord Harrow. I am engaged to be wed."

Olivia's arched brows flattened into a dark frown. "It is not yet official," she countered. "My sister will tell Lord Randolf that she made a mistake."

Susanna curled her teeth back. "La, Olivia, how you carry on. Of course I shall not cry off. I have every intention of marrying the man."

"You are only doing so because he is rich."

"It is as good a reason as any." Susanna came to Jack and held out her hands. "But you should not be privy to our little family quarrels. May I ring for tea? I hear you sent us a perfectly enormous goose for Christmas. And oranges as well. How extraordinarily kind of you." She gave a shrill laugh. "I shall be able to pay you back in kind next year."

"Susanna, you hate the man," Olivia hissed.

Mrs. Clarke remained perfectly composed. There was anger and fear in her eyes, but her veneer of breeding covered it well. Jack could see now that the Faraday sisters were not so different from one another after all. They were all abominably stubborn.

"Nonetheless," Susanna said regally, "I will marry him." She smiled then, the perfect London hostess. "Now, the tea. Molly has made a lovely cake. Shall I ask her to bring it? I'll just go ask her to make up a tray. Perhaps you wouldn't mind saying hello to the boys? They have grown so fond of you." She swept out of the room.

Olivia remained standing, staring after her sister with an expression of pain. She looked around the room at her family for support, but Frederica was looking mulish and her father merely continued whittling a piece of wood that was slowly taking the shape of a dog. Olivia avoided his own eyes.

"I know Randolf," Mr. Faraday said quietly from his chair by the kiln. "Good man. Bit high in the instep, but decent for all that. Hired me once to engineer some improvements. Had a lake he wanted drained. Once I'd presented him with my plans, Baxter came in and offered to do it more cheaply. But Randolf stayed with me. I've heard people say he's arrogant. And I suppose he is. Certainly not a warm man. But for all that, he's decent."

Olivia stared at her father, bemused.

"Randolf told me that he was in love with your sister," Jack said quietly. "Surely that counts for something."

She turned on him, suddenly angry. "No. It does not count for enough. Not if she cannot return his affection." She went to stoke up the fire to a more savage heat. Each jab of the tongs was accomplished with a great deal more force than was necessary. "I can't let her do this," she said at last.

He felt the pain in his rib again. "Weren't you prepared to make the same sacrifice this afternoon?" he asked.

She swung around to look at him with a glare that should have turned him to stone. He saw her lips tremble as though she would speak, but she turned back to the fire without a word.

"Where's my tea?" Mr. Faraday demanded.

Frederica put her small hand in Jack's. "Perhaps *you* could go talk to Susanna?" she suggested in a whisper. "You could find out if she truly hates Randolf. Perhaps she is merely a little indifferent. In which case it would probably be all right if she married him. She might get over it. Don't you think?"

"No," Olivia said quickly.

Jack turned to her. "Why not?" he asked. "I am happy

to speak with Mrs. Clarke. I believe I am reasonably impartial."

"Because, because," she stammered incoherently. "Because she'll probably end up marrying you instead."

It was his turn to look at her in disbelief. Good Lord, but this was turning into a French farce. The woman was obviously addled. Perhaps it was the heat. He took out his handkerchief and mopped his brow. "What the devil are you talking about?"

Her face was growing pink. "She thinks she must marry someone in order to help our family. And you seem to feel the need to do something for us. In two minutes you will have decided that if you marry each other it will solve everything!"

The pain in his rib suddenly felt a thousand times better. "And what is wrong with that, Olivia?" he asked, gravely. "As you say, it would solve a multitude of problems."

"It would not," she bristled. "It would be a terrible idea. You are not suited for each other. It is the wrong reason to marry."

"And what is the right reason to marry?" His tone was light, but he could not draw a breath until she answered.

She stared at him, a look that was almost like anguish on her face. "I-I-I don't see why anyone has to marry. It's ridiculous. We will be fine without anyone throwing themselves at anyone else."

He forced himself to shrug as though it was entirely immaterial how this played out. "Susanna does not wish to marry Randolf, yet she has indicated that my suit would be acceptable. Of course I am not an earl, but I am under the impression that she does not find me quite so odious as Lord Randolf. Why should we not throw our lots in together and in doing so, make things better for those we care about?"

"No," she said quickly. "No."

He felt the same thrill he felt with a winning hand in a game of hazard. There might be hope.

His heart pounding, he flung himself into the chair furthest from the fire with what he hoped was a look of unconcern. "I might remind you that at the moment, your sister is already engaged to someone else. It is folly to distress yourself over a marriage that is unlikely to happen."

"I am not distressed!" she snapped. "Papa, you must tell Susanna she cannot marry Lord Randolf. Or Lord Harrow."

Her father shot her a look of mild disbelief. "In my experience, I have found that each of my daughters has done exactly as she wishes." He turned to Jack. "Dashed stubborn chits."

"They are indeed, sir."

"But you can't help but like 'em."

He laughed then, particularly when he saw Olivia's expression of sputtering annoyance. "No, sir," he said with the first real smile he'd had all day, "you can't help but like them."

Nineteen

The dowager Lady Harrow looked over the Faraday sisters as though they were a plague of rats who had multiplied. "Ah," she said with the chilliest of smiles, "I see my nephew has seen fit to invite *all* of you to our Christmas Eve Yule ball." She cast a glance around her ballroom, lavishly ornamented with Christmas greenery and the cream of Bedfordshire society. The dowager obviously hoped they would blend in with the former and stay out of the way of the latter.

"I was included on the invitation," Frederica piped up defiantly.

"How kind of him," the dowager replied. "I would have thought an invitation to the children's ball on Twelfth Night quite sufficient."

Amelia Westhaven, beautiful and fashionable as always, came over to them, her hands extended. "How lovely to see all of you. Oh Aunt, how kind of you to invite my favorite friends."

Olivia looked at the woman in surprise. After all, Lady Westhaven hadn't given her a glance during her Season. Jack's sister had been kind enough at the Yule log party, but friends? She gave her a tentative smile, unsure. The dowager looked similarly stymied.

"How fashionable you look, Miss Frederica," Amelia

continued warmly. "I shouldn't have recognized you. Will you be making your come-out soon?"

Frederica, instantly won over, blushed prettily. With her hair coiffed at Susanna's expert direction and her gown newly turned and trimmed for the occasion, she did look quite grown-up. Olivia felt a small pang of loss.

"Not for a few years," Susanna answered for her. "She is not but thirteen. But when she does, I will be sponsoring her. After I have married Lord Randolf."

Unlike their younger sister, Susanna was not in her best looks tonight. Despite the glory of the much-discussed blush gown, her eyes were accented with dark circles, her lips nearly as pale as her cheeks. Olivia pressed her sister's limp hand, but she pulled away.

Susanna had sacrificed everything for them. She'd had the courage to do what Olivia herself had not.

She'd had the chance to marry Harrow, a voice in Olivia's head reminded her cruelly. But she'd been too proud to accept what she'd thought had been charity. She was beginning to get used to feeling as though she was wearing a leaden corset.

Lady Westhaven clasped her hands. "Lord Randolf? Oh, how romantic. He's the most dashing man, is he not? So dark and mysterious." She gave Susanna an arch smile. "And I'm not the least bit surprised to find he's won you. I've seen the way he looks at you."

Susanna looked caught between bemused and flattered, Frederica seemed intrigued, and the dowager appeared downright bewildered. Lady Westhaven beamed at them, then linked her arm with Olivia's and led her away, as though they were indeed the best of friends.

"Well, I think that did the trick," she said, looking over her shoulder in satisfaction.

"I beg your pardon?" Olivia said, drawing herself up stiffly. She felt like a crow in the company of a swan. Lady Westhaven was the picture of fashion in her graceful, dark-blue gown.

She herself wore a simple gown from her Season, now two years out of date. The pale gold dress was appropriate for an unmarried woman, but she had never felt that it flattered her. Even retrimmed with sparkling glass beads, it was nothing memorable. With her washed-out eyes, hair, and skin, she might as well be entirely transparent. And in this sumptuously dressed crowd, she apparently was.

Harrow's sister grinned. "Your sister seems unhappy to be marrying Lord Randolf. But I believe it is only because she sees it as a duty and not a challenge."

Olivia withdrew her arm. "I hope my sister's future has not become common gossip."

"Oh, don't be prickly," the woman said, not the least bit daunted by her lofty tone. "It's obvious from her face how she feels. Though I'm glad she mentioned the engagement in front of my aunt. You should have seen the expression on her face!"

"I—"

"And I thought Susanna might need some encouragement."

Olivia knew she should not have come tonight. One couldn't enjoy a Christmas Eve ball when one was suffering from lead-corset syndrome. She forced herself to smile politely at Harrow's kindly meddling sister. "Susanna will not marry Randolf," she explained patiently. "She detests him."

Lady Westhaven looked across the room to where her

husband was gesturing to her to join him. Her smile was something joyful, private, luminous. She then turned back to Olivia. "Randolf is a good man. And he cares very much for your sister. I believe he can make her love him."

If only it were possible to make someone love you. She looked around the room but did not see Lady Westhaven's brother.

The woman looked at her gloved hands for a moment, suddenly serious. "Miss Faraday, you have every reason not to like me. I know we met during your Season two years ago, and that I made little effort to get to know you. I apologize for that, for I know you were perhaps, a bit—"

"Unpopular?" Olivia supplied, drawing herself up.

"Left out," Lady Westhaven said. She bit her lip. "It wasn't fair of me. I wish I had known we had more in common."

Olivia felt the old defensiveness coming back. They had nothing in common. Lady Westhaven was beautiful and rich. She was neither of those things. All they had ever had in common was her brother. And now they did not have that. "I don't believe we do have anything in common, Lady Westhaven."

"Call me Amelia, please." She smiled, her open face sincere. "And you are wrong. We have a great deal in common. We both enjoy living in the country. We both care about seeing that our respective estates are properly taken care of. I have put quite a lot of effort into learning about how to manage Crownhaven. A large portion of my knowledge came from your father's writings. He is a great man, you know. One of the greatest agriculturalists of our age."

Unwillingly, Olivia felt her reserve thawing. "Yes," she said. "I know."

"Jack talks constantly of the improvements your father has made. Would you mind very much introducing Hunter and me to him? Hunter has a small obsession with the mangel-wurzel, and I know he would be delighted to ask your father his opinion. We enjoyed his article last year in the *British Journal of Agricultural Sciences*."

"Yes, of course, Lady West—Amelia," Olivia managed to stammer. How humbling to be constantly surprised. She had condemned the Westhavens as decorative objects only. Instead they were obviously intelligent people whom her father would greatly enjoy meeting. "I must tell you, though—" She felt her throat growing tight. "My father is not as he was. He suffers from, well—he has become rather senile."

Amelia's hand pressed her own. "I'm sorry to hear that," she said simply. "That must be difficult."

Oddly, that seemed the right thing to say. Olivia smiled. It was rather unfortunate the woman was Jack Harrow's sister. They were unlikely to meet again. Jack's last gesture of generosity in giving her father the deed to the house this morning had signaled the end of his connection with the Faraday family.

Like a bird, Amelia gathered herself together in preparation for flight. "I must go to Hunter. Look, here is Jack!" Her brows flew up in an expression of exaggerated surprise. "Jack, I'm certain you're looking for someone to dance with. And here is Miss Faraday."

Olivia felt a prickling rush of panic. She didn't want to see Jack just yet. Of course she must face him. But not yet. And certainly she didn't wish to dance with him. She tried to compose her face into a suitably impassive expression.

Amelia grabbed her brother's hand, linked it with Olivia's, and then flitted off into the crowd.

Lord Harrow gave an uncomfortable laugh and withdrew his hand. "Forgive my sister. She has an uncontrollable urge to meddle. I believe she thinks that since she made a success of her own marriage, despite its disastrous beginnings, that she is an expert in all relationships."

"She was only trying to convince me that Randolf is not a bad match for my sister," she said, inexplicably able to speak only to Harrow's cravat. Her corset, now not only leaden, seemed to be growing more constrictive as well.

"Just because he is not as charming as I am doesn't mean he isn't a good man." He grinned. "Even your father said so."

As always, when he set out to needle her, she could not help but rise to the bait. "My father never said you were charming."

"Perhaps not," he said, impervious to her attempt at scorn. "In fact, I seem to recall he always calls me a wastrel. But he did say that Randolf is a right one. Both proof of his excellent judgment."

He really was an impossible man.

But one could get over being in love with someone who was impossible, surely. Possibly the first step required the ability to draw a full breath.

Jack idly watched the room. He appeared perfectly at home in this luxury. He was not in the least bit impressed by the miles of greenery, the crystal icicles, the bouquets of bright berries and velvet ribbons that decorated the room. Even the smell of the room was luxurious with the scent of beeswax, ginger, and cloves. His foot was tapping lightly in time to the lively waltz.

"Will you dance?" he asked, as though he'd only just recalled that she was beside him.

"I thought you hated dancing," she replied tartly.

"I do," he said. His gaze rose above her head. "But it seems our options are limited."

She looked up. Good heavens. Another kissing bough. She couldn't live through another passionless kiss from him. She scuttled away as though the detestable mistletoe might fall down and crush her. "I will dance."

He swept her into the circle of the waltz with languid grace. Did the man do everything perfectly? She tried to recall that he hadn't known a mangel-wurzel from a swede when she had first met him.

Now, of course, he did. Now he knew a great deal. He didn't need her at all.

"I was hoping you could do me a favor, Olivia."

"What?" What could she possibly do for him? She'd offered him everything, and he'd refused her. Shame burnt her ears.

"I was hoping you and I could go riding with North. Show him the estate. Before I go back to London."

"Of course," she said in a hollow voice. She knew he'd be leaving, but so soon? He was going back to London and she would not see him again. She had known it would happen. She'd even gone as far as to hope that it would ease her heartache. But now, hearing it, she only felt loss.

"We will also need to discuss future improvements he might make. I would like your father's opinion."

"Indeed. I am sure he will give it willingly."

He looked down into her face, assessing her set expression. He frowned. "Can we not be friends, Olivia?" he asked gently.

Did he have to make this harder? "Of course," she said brightly. "Of course we can be friends."

She knew he could see right through her false cheer, but he smiled anyway. "I have always enjoyed your company. Even when it was patently obvious I irritated you."

"Nonsense," she said, her voice catching in her throat.

He swung her into a turn. They were in the center of the room now, under the bright gold glow of the chandelier swagged with greenery. She looked around, willing herself to remember every beautiful detail of this last glimpse of his glittering world.

"And I will always be grateful to you for your instructions," he said. "I enjoyed it a great deal more than you would guess, for all my complaining." He laughed. "And I may have even learned something."

He was trying to jolly her out of her reserve, but she still found that she did not quite know what to say. This was the end. "I'm certain the estate will flourish under your care," she choked out.

He was nodding and smiling at other couples as they waltzed by. Miss Eggart caught his eye and gave him a flirtatious simper. "I was thinking we might sow flax in the fields by the shearing barn," he said, accidentally pulling her closer as he moved her into a turn.

"Flax?" she repeated, astounded. "Those fields are too wet for flax. And they've got another season left in the soil for oats. We could do flax the year after that. If we were able to get it to drain better, which I am not at all certain of."

She looked up at him and saw that he was grinning that impossible grin. She resisted the urge to drive a knuckle into his bicep as she used to do to Christopher when he irritated her. Oh, but Christopher would have liked Jack. "You are mocking me," she said, her chin rising.

"But you give the most remarkable set-downs." His voice was low and close to her ear.

Was he flirting with her? Impossible. "If you have chosen to dance with me only to provoke me," she said, pretending asperity for old time's sake, "I shall not speak at all."

He seemed unperturbed. "Then I will merely enjoy looking at you."

She felt herself blushing. First of all, men did not flirt with Olivia Faraday. Second, Jack Harrow, bluff, care-for-nobody, sportingman Jack Harrow, didn't flirt. Thirdly, it would be strange, if not even cruel, to flirt with a woman one had rejected out of hand only this morning.

"I like what you're wearing," he said. "You look all gold and sparkling. Like a glass of champagne."

She rolled her eyes, but felt her blood race faster all the same. "I suppose you meant that as a compliment."

"I'm not very good with compliments," he admitted wryly. "But I like champagne. So what I meant was that you look . . . well, you look pretty."

She pulled away from him. "You're confusing me."

"You shouldn't be confused," he said. "I've always thought you were pretty. Even when you give me the gorgon glare. I've come to rather enjoy it."

She was dancing with the most handsome man in the room. And he had just told her that he'd always thought her pretty. She should be the happiest woman in the world. Instead she felt as though the wretched corset was about to squeeze her in half.

"You are being unkind," she said with a scowl. "Everything was settled between us. Everything was done. Let us leave it the way it was."

He sighed. "I'm very difficult, aren't I? But it would have made things a dashed bit easier if you'd only accepted my proposal the first time around."

Her heart stopped. She was sure of it. In another moment Jack would be in the embarrassing situation of trying to drag a limp body off the dance floor. "You were only proposing out of pity," she said breathlessly, trying to muster up the requisite amount of scorn.

"Pity *you?*" he exclaimed. "I should never have the courage."

She tried to summon up a witty retort, but the expression on his face was making it hard to breathe, never mind talk. She was uncomfortably aware of losing control. She looked around the room, desperate for another topic of conversation.

She caught a glimpse of Susanna's blush-and-silver ball gown as her sister slipped from the room. Randolf, his expression ominously dark, strode after her.

"Will you excuse me?" she said, feeling a sudden sense of foreboding. "I need to go to my sister."

"We are in the middle of a dance." Jack's arm tightened around her.

She felt the breathlessness again. Only this morning he'd said clearly that he would not marry her, and yet he was looking at her in a way that suggested that if she threw herself at him as she had at the Yule log outing, he might not object. She put those thoughts from her mind. "I must go to her," she said.

What was Susanna up to? Had she finally gotten enough sense to call off the engagement? Randolf looked none too pleased. Surely he wouldn't become violent, but . . .

With calm skill, Jack maneuvered them closer to the door through which the couple had departed. Then, without a word, he took Olivia's hand and whisked her out of the room.

"You don't have to come with me," she whispered, when they were alone in the empty corridor. But he said nothing and merely started down the hallway.

It was dim—nothing like the brilliance of the ballroom. The candles had burned low in their sconces and cast shifting shadows over the pattern of the gold silk walls. The muted noise from the ballroom made the rest of the house seem strangely desolate.

In front of her, Jack was peeking into open doorways and pressing his ear to any he found closed. She watched as his face lit up and gestured silently at a closed door.

He didn't have to do this. He didn't have to do any of this for her. He'd already done so much. She thought of the deed, the letters to Eton, that wretched, darling goose.

"Jack," she said quietly. He gestured for her silence, but she went up to him and continued anyway. "I know now isn't the time, but well, I just wanted to tell you that I am glad you hired Mr. North. I am confident that he is the perfect person to continue my father's works. You were right. My father cannot go on with his work. My sisters and I must enjoy our time with him, but realize that he will never again be the man he was. I was wrong to insist that it was your duty to keep him on."

He looked at her for a moment, saying nothing. Then, to her surprise, he put a hand on either side of her face. "You're a remarkable woman, Olivia Faraday," he said softly. "You are loyal and loving and fierce and true. I know you hold me responsible for much of what has happened to your family. And I don't blame you. But I want you to know how much I admire you and your devotion to your family. I want you to know how much I wish the circumstances that pitted us against each other had been different."

His green eyes held no laughter now. Still and grave, they burned into her. "No matter how things end between us," he said, "I want you to remember that."

Twenty

A rise in the level of voices inside the room drew Jack's attention, and he reluctantly released Olivia. She was concerned about her sister, he reminded himself. This was not the moment to court her.

"I don't have to marry anyone!" Susanna was saying, her voice sharp and overloud. "How dare you accuse me of marrying for money."

Olivia tensed. She reached out and took the door handle, ready to burst in, the savior.

There was the low murmur of Randolf's voice, and then Susanna, shrill again. "I don't care. I don't. My father has money. I found it. I don't have to marry you."

Jack put his hand on Olivia's shoulder. She was still, not even breathing. He looked down at her, but her eyes were fixed on the door. She turned the door handle and noiselessly pushed it open.

"In the mattress," Susanna was saying. "I found it this afternoon when I was cleaning up after the fire. Papa forgot he'd hidden it there. It isn't much. But it will ensure that Olivia and Frederica have dowries. At least something."

Olivia maneuvered herself so she could see through the crack in the door. She was entirely unaware that she was pressed against him, squeezed between his body and the doorframe, the white silk flowers in her hair tickling his nose.

"Susanna," Randolf said calmly, "my feelings for you have nothing to do with your financial circumstances. If you accepted me only because of my money, or only because of my family, for God's sake, I release you from our engagement."

Randolf came into their field of view as he turned away. Jack felt a painful twist of sympathy for the man. It was obvious from his expression that the man was deeply in love with Susanna Clarke. Randolf dragged a hand across his forehead, visibly trying to compose himself.

"You are a cold man," Susanna was saying. "I cannot believe you care one way or another whether I marry you." But her voice shook as she said it.

Randolf turned on her then. "How can you say that?" He crossed the room to her. "Susanna, I am not a man who loves lightly. Perhaps you mistake my natural reserve for coldness, and if that is so, be assured that my feelings for you are far more passionate than I would willingly admit. Particularly when I suspect you do not return my feelings."

He drew a tight breath. "If you cannot love me, tell me to go away. I will do it, my love. But if you can—if you think you might grow to care for me, then give me a chance."

He must have seen something in her expression, for he instantly took her into his arms and kissed her. Susanna's hands tightened on his back. They pulled apart for a moment, their voices dropping to whispers, then he kissed her again. There was a long silence, in which Susanna made it obvious that she was indeed quite willing to give him a chance.

To Jack's surprise, Olivia stepped back, bumping into him. His hands reached out to steady her, but he stopped himself.

"We must go," Olivia said, her voice the barest whisper. She pulled the door closed. Dash it all, just when things were getting interesting.

She moved away from him, taking with her the perfume and warmth of her presence. He sensed that she didn't want him intruding on her thoughts at the moment, but he followed her anyway. She was standing at the end of the hallway in front of a large mirror, her hands bracing herself on the ornate, onyx-topped side table in front of it.

"Is it true?" he asked quietly.

Her shoulder blades moved together and apart as she sighed. The shift of her bones under the skin made her appear both tempting and vulnerable. He longed to hold her. "About the money?" she said. "I don't know." She continued to stand there, staring at her hands on the table.

Her profile was perfect. How could he ever have thought her less than beautiful? How could he ever have thought that mobile, expressive face cold? "Does it matter?"

Her eyes caught his in the mirror. She must have sensed that he meant more than the obvious: her family, their welfare. "I don't know," she said.

He spoke to her reflection, unable to face her in front of him in real life. "If money was not an issue, would you reconsider me?"

She did not lift her eyes again. Then, just when the silence had become unbearable, "I refused your proposal because you do not love me. Not because of your money."

The painful tightness in his lungs prevented him from breathing. "And yet you asked me to marry you yesterday because of my money. Because your sister had saddled herself with a loveless match."

Olivia's eyes met his in the mirror. "No. I didn't know about Susanna's engagement when I asked—"

He wasn't sure if he could believe her. And now, if what Susanna said was true, he had neither her poverty nor Susanna's misalliance to tempt Olivia into marriage with him.

"But now you see that Susanna's marriage is perhaps not such a sacrifice after all," he said. "And now with your father's money and Lord Randolf's, you will have school for the boys, a Season for your sister, all the things you would not let me give you."

She stood there, staring mutely at him.

"I don't blame you, Olivia. I don't." He tried to smile, but had the suspicion that it didn't look quite right. "In fact, I should thank you. I, who have always had everything I wanted, have now discovered what it is like to want. I run an estate now, I'm a respectable viscount. A viscount who throws blasted Christmas balls, for God's sake. I suppose it is healthy to have experienced unrequieted love as well."

He fell back a step and crossed his arms to keep himself from touching her. "But dash it all, Olivia! Did you have to make it harder this morning? Did you have to tempt me? Asking me to marry you while making it clear that you were only doing it for the money?"

Her skirts hissed against his boots as she whirled around to face him. "No," she said again, forcefully this time. "No. That wasn't it." He saw her slender throat move as she swallowed. "You give me too much credit."

They stared at each other for a moment. He was at

sea. What the devil did "no" mean? Did it mean he could take her in his arms as he wished? Or did it mean he should take himself off and drown his sorrows in the nearest lake of brandy?

"I asked you—" she drew an uneven breath, "I asked you to marry me because I—" another breath, more unsteady than the last, "because I found I had made a mistake before."

"A mistake," he echoed stupidly. "I didn't think you ever made mistakes."

"Well, I did."

His heart was a painful knot in his chest. He manfully resisted the urge to crush her in an embrace. "Was it the kind of mistake that might perhaps have led you to say, 'No, I hate you and everything you represent,' instead of 'Yes, Jack Harrow, I will condescend to marry you?'"

She smiled faintly. "Not exactly."

His heart fell. "'Yes, Jack Harrow, I can tolerate you, and marriage to you would be an acceptable alternative to being savaged by wild dogs?'" he suggested weakly.

She gave a reluctant laugh. "No."

"No?" he choked. "Perhaps you meant to say, 'No, I hate you, everything you represent, many things you don't represent, and I sincerely hope a large rock falls on your head?'"

He'd once gambled several hundred pounds on the turn of a card, and lost. That sick feeling was nothing to this.

She wrapped her arms around her waist in a strange, protective gesture, as though her own vulnerability was painful. He himself felt raw. "No," she said. "Not that."

"Then—"

She looked at him, then abruptly dropped her gaze to

the carpet. "I meant to say I would be proud to marry you."

"Proud?" he echoed incredulously. "No one has ever been proud of me."

She drew herself up, the old indignant Olivia again. "Well, that is simply ridiculous. How could they not be? Look at what you've accomplished. You learned every inch of this estate. Far better than anyone could have hoped. My father himself said you're not half the wastrel he thought. And look at how the neighbors like you. They look up to you. How could they not?"

"You're proud of me?" he said, a foolish grin creeping across his face.

Her chin rose. "Yes. Yes, I am."

"But being proud of someone is not the same as loving them." He caught her chin in his hand and looked down at her. "I'm a very greedy fellow. I want you to love me."

To his surprise, his gorgon blushed. "I do." She looked up at him and smiled, suddenly confident. "I do."

He felt like his horse had won at Ascot. No, better. A thousand times better. He resisted the urge to shout his triumph only because it would mean releasing her from his arms. "And you'll marry me? Money, title, and all?"

She was still flushed, but she beamed at him. "Yes."

He kissed her then, first a joyous sealing of the bargain, then another of promise, and yet another of passion. Just when he was considering the necessity of bolting into the ballroom and ordering Reverend Eggart to marry them on the spot, they were interrupted by a blissful sigh from behind a potted plant.

"Frederica?" Olivia called out suspiciously.

After a brief twitching of leaves, her sister appeared.

"Susanna is kissing her earl," she announced, smug. "She didn't hate him after all." Her grin broadened. "And it looks as though you might have changed your mind about the viscount as well."

Olivia said nothing, but merely rose onto her toes and kissed him again.

Frederica looked them over with an eagle eye. "I suppose you will both get married. Though of course Susanna has the higher title, and that will please her. And once you are married ladies of fortune, it will mean, of course, that Papa will be taken care of, and I shall have my Season and the boys will go to school, and Susanna will stop being desperate, and you will not be quite so cross." She listed the benefits off on her fingers.

"And next year we shall have an even grander Christmas." She crossed her arms over her chest and looked quite satisfied. "I told you my Christmas wishes always came true."

ABOUT THE AUTHOR

Catherine Blair lives in The Netherlands. She is currently working on her next Zebra regency romance, A NOTORIOUS LADY, which will be published in 2004. Catherine loves to hear from readers and you may write to her c/o Zebra Books. Please include a self-addressed, stamped envelope if you wish a response.